John S. Ogilvie

The Press Prize Recipes for Meats, Vegetables, Bread, and Pastry

John S. Ogilvie

The Press Prize Recipes for Meats, Vegetables, Bread, and Pastry

ISBN/EAN: 9783337377595

Printed in Europe, USA, Canada, Australia, Japan

Cover: Foto ©Andreas Hilbeck / pixelio.de

More available books at **www.hansebooks.com**

THE "PRESS"

PRIZE RECIPES

FOR

MEATS, VEGETABLES, BREAD, AND PASTRY.

*Being a Collection of Recipes furnished by the Lady
Readers of the " Press," competing for the Five
Prizes of One Dozen Solid Silver Spoons
each, offered for the Best Methods
of Preparing Staple Dishes.*

THE RECIPES ARE PRACTICAL AND ECONOMICAL.

...ISHER,

...BASH AVENUE, CHICAGO.

ONE HUNDRED
PRIZE DINNERS;

OR,

HOW TO PROVIDE A GOOD DINNER FOR FOUR PERSONS FOR ONE DOLLAR.

*Compiled from the columns of the New York "Press,"
the publishers of which offered a Prize of
$100.00 for the best Bill of
Fare offered.*

———

**AN INVALUABLE GUIDE FOR PERSONS OF MODERATE INCOME
TO PROVIDE GOOD FOOD AT A LOW PRICE.**

———

This valuable book, which every lady should have, will be sent by mail, post-paid, on receipt of **25 cts.**

Lady Agents Wanted to Sell it.

A copy can be sold in *every house.* Address orders and applications for agency to

J. S. OGILVIE, Publisher,

57 Rose Street, New York.

CONTENTS.

BREAD.

CAKE, PASTRY, AND PUDDINGS.

MEATS.

THE "PRESS" PRIZE RECIPES.

1. OLD-FASHIONED YANKEE BREAD.

Sift two pounds of best flour on bread tray. Make a hollow place in the center and drop in a piece of lard the size of a tablespoon. Dissolve one yeast cake in a little warm water and put that in with the lard, and one teaspoonful of salt and half a tea-cup of sugar. Then mix it with lukewarm water until it is thick, and turn it out on your molding-board and mold it till it shines and does not stick to the board. You cannot mold it too much. Then put it back on the tray. Cover it with a cloth, not very heavy, and put it in a warm place till morning. When it becomes very light put it on the board again and mold it down till it is solid. Set it in a warm place, and as soon as it rises nicely mold it again, and put it in buttered pans and bake immediately. This takes a little time, but you will have good bread.

2. BREAD.

It is impossible to make good bread without good-yeast, an article hard to be got. As a preliminary to "directions for bread making" here is a recipe which has been used since 1875, and never known to fail in producing good yeast if properly observed.

YEAST.—Put a small handful of hops to steep in a scant pint of boiling water. Grate one teacupful of raw potatoes, put it into a pitcher or bowl; upon this put one half cup of granulated sugar, the same of salt, one teaspoonful of ground ginger, and two quarts of boiling water; then strain and add the hot water, a coffee-cup full, boiling hot. Stir all together, and when lukewarm add one and a half dissolved hard yeast cakes, which must be sweet, or the yeast will be spoiled. After twelve hours, if kept in a warm place, the mixture will rise and be covered with a thick froth. It must then be put into glass jars, such as are used for fruit, and kept sealed from the air. If placed in refrigerator this will be sweet three weeks. Enough should be reserved for raising next time. Half of the quantities above are sufficient for the use of a small family.

Now for the bread. First, the sponge. Use one boiled potato, mashed through a colander, one pint lukewarm water, one small teacupful yeast, and flour sufficient to make stiff batter; beat hard for a few minutes and set in warm place to rise. In the Spring of the year it is well to make this sponge about 2 P.M. It will then be light about 9 P.M., when the bread may be mixed and be ready for baking early in the morning.

To make the dough, put about three quarts of

flour in bread-pan, make a hole in the center, put
therein for shortening a lump (of the size of hen's
egg) of lard, butter or (what is better) roast-beef
drippings ; pour thereon slowly a cupful boiling
water, all the while mashing it with a wooden
spoon ; then add a pint of milk and a tablespoonful of salt, and lastly your light sponge. Stir all
with spoon till too thick to be stirred longer, then
knead with hands, the while adding flour to make
the dough (if Plant's flour is used the dough must
be stiff ; if new process flour, not stiff) ; then put
the mass on bread board and work it for at least
twenty minutes, slashing it meanwhile with a sharp
knife. Now put in bread-pan and leave all night
in a warm place. In the morning mold into loaves
and place in bread-pans ; when light bake, which
will require from three-quarters to an hour, according to heat of oven.

If hot biscuit are wished for breakfast, take as
much light dough as required, work into it a small
piece of shortening, make into rolls or forms, brush
the tops with melted butter, and place in a warming oven a few minutes to hasten the raising process, then bake.

3. BREAD.

About 5 o'clock in the afternoon take a pint of
warm milk with a little salt in it, stir flour enough
to make a thin sponge and add two thirds cup of
yeast ; let stand in a warm place until about 9.30
or a little later, then dissolve quarter teaspoon of
soda in a little warm water and stir in, adding flour

enough to make a solid loaf; do not mix in any
more flour than necessary to keep from sticking, as
there is danger of getting too stiff; knead it about
fifteen minutes, then cover well and set near the
fire on the table until morning. In the morning
open it with your hands and mix just enough to
get the gas out, put it into a loaf, let stand in a
warm place; when light bake in a moderate oven
from thirty to forty minutes, according to size of
loaf and heat of oven. Be careful and not let it
get too light.

4. BREAD.

Take seven pounds of flour and sieve it in a large
wooden or earthenware bowl. Take a piece of
butter, size of an egg, half a teacupful of sugar, a
large handful of salt, and mix it through the flour,
dry. Take one yeast cake and break it up in a teacupful of lukewarm water and let it dissolve; pour
it into the flour. Take a quart and a pint of lukewarm water (for winter, cold for summer) and pour
it in the flour, mixing as poured in. Mix until not
too stiff. If necessary a little more flour or water
is used. Cover up with bread cloth and set in
warm place to rise. Mix at 10 o'clock P.M., and in
the morning it is ready to mold. Take a little
flour on a pastry board and mold it up and put in
greased pans. Then set in a warm place for half
an hour or more for it to rise again. Bake one
hour in a slow oven. When done set it to cool, but
don't cover it up, as the moisture wants to come
out. This makes four good sized loaves of bread.

5. BATH BUNS.

Four large coffee cups of sifted flour, four tablespoons powdered sugar and one teaspoon salt, all
mixed together.   One compressed yeast cake, dissolved in a little warm water; two eggs well beaten;
one coffee cup warm milk, the same of warm water;
stir all the liquids together, with butter size of an
English walnut dissolved in them; them mix into
your flour as for ordinary bread.   For 6 o'clock
Sunday tea mix at 8 A.M.; let rise till 3 P.M.   Then
do not knead, but pick off pieces size of a large
egg and roll round between the palms of your
hands.   Put in a well-greased dripping-pan, an
inch apart, and let rise again till 5 P.M.; then bake
in a quick hot oven.   Just before they are done
brush with molasses and water, and serve with
powdered sugar sprinkled over them.   A very good
recipe for hot cross buns.

6. SPLIT BISCUITS.

These are made for tea when bread has been
baked in the morning.   Take one pint of risen
dough, and add to it one scant pint of milk, two
tablespoonfuls of butter, four of sugar, one teaspoonful of salt, and two well beaten eggs.   Mix
all the ingredients in a bowl, cutting the dough
with a knife.   After the mixing add a generous
quart of flour.   Knead the dough well and let it
stand in a warm place for six hours, when it should
be a perfect sponge.   Work it down well at the end
of that time.   Sprinkle the molding board with

flour, and, turning the dough upon the board, roll
it down to the thickness of about one fourth of an
inch.   Dip a biscuit cutter in flour and cut up the
dough with it.   Place half of the cakes in buttered
pans.   Spread a little soft butter on each cake.
Take fresh cakes from the board and put them on
top of those already in pans.   Cover and set away
in rather a cool place to rise, and when they are
about double their original size (it will take about
two hours) bake in a rather hot oven for half an
hour.   This amount will make two good sized pans
of biscuits.

7. ROLLS.

Measure out two quarts of flour, scald one pint
of milk, when lukewarm add one half cup of granulated sugar, one half cup of yeast, one half teaspoon soda, and butter size of an egg.   Mix in flour
enough to make a sponge, let it raise ten or twelve
hours.   When light knead in the rest of the flour
and let it raise again till light, then knead about
ten minutes.   Roll out one half inch thick, cut into
circles the size of a small tea saucer, spread with
butter, double the buttered surface together, and
let them rise a few hours.   This is not much work,
but is very delicious.

8. BOSTON TEA OR COFFEE CAKES.

One well beaten egg, two tablespoons sugar, one
cup sweet milk, two cups flour, three teaspoons
baking powder, one tablespoon melted butter, a
little salt.   Bake in a quick oven in muffin rings.

9. TEA BISCUIT.

One quart flour, three teaspoonfuls baking powder, one teaspoonful salt, one tablespoonful butter, one pint milk. Sift the flour and baking powder together into a mixing bowl; add salt, butter, and lastly the milk; mix thoroughly and quickly with the hands into a soft dough. The more quickly this is done the lighter the biscuit will be. Flour the hands, break off bits of the dough the size you wish, and quickly roll into any shape. Bake in a quick oven twenty minutes.

10. HOME MADE CRULLERS.

To nine tablespoonfuls of granulated sugar add four tablespoonfuls of melted butter. Beat well together, then add three well beaten eggs, two heaping teaspoonfuls of baking powder, one teacupful of milk, one teaspoonful of salt, half a small grated nutmeg. Mix with flour just stiff enough to roll nicely on board. Cut out same as cookies with a hole in center. Fry in sweet lard. They are nearly perfect. This recipe will make forty crullers. Roll in powdered sugar when slightly cool.

11. CORN CAKE.

Take one cup of corn meal, one cup of flour, one and a half teaspoons of baking powder, a half teaspoon of salt, two tablespoons of sugar, sifted three times; one tablespoonful of butter, two eggs well beaten, a cup and a half of cold water. Have the

tin or muffin rings well greased and piping hot.
Bake in a quick oven.

12. SNOWBALL BISCUITS.

To four cups flour add two tablespoonfuls of
butter, rub it into the flour, sift in four teaspoons-
ful of baking powder, stir together lightly till
thoroughly mixed; then add one and a half cups
of sweet milk, stir all together quickly, roll in a
ball, with as little handling as possible, roll out
about one half inch thick and bake in a hot oven.

13. BUCKWHEAT GRIDDLE CAKES.

Three cups buckwheat meal, three cups milk, one
half cake of yeast, one small teaspoonful salt, one
half teaspoonful soda.   Scald the milk, to prevent
souring; when cool dissolve yeast in it, and stir
into the meal; mix at night and stand in a warm
place to rise; in the morning dissolve, add soda
and beat up the batter thoroughly; fry on very hot
griddle, but not hot enough to burn the cakes; fry
in cakes the size of the griddle and butter and
sugar them in layers, not serving until they are all
fried, and then cutting as you would a pie, or fry
in tablespoonfuls and have them served as soon as
fried.   For dressing use maple sugar, shaved fine,
with or without butter, or butter and powdered
sugar.

14. PARKER HOUSE ROLLS.

One quart of flour, a pinch of salt, one pint of
milk, one and one half cups of butter, one third

cup of sugar, one forth of a yeast cake. Make over night. In the morning roll out about one half inch thick and cut out round. Butter one half and the other half fold over the buttered part Place them in a baking tin and allow them to rise all day. Bake about fifteen minutes for tea.

15. FRENCH ROLLS.

Take two quarts of flour and rub half a cup of butter well into it. Warm a pint and a half of milk (some flour will take more) and dissolve a cake of compressed yeast and three tablespoonfuls of sugar in it, with two eggs well beaten, and large teaspoon of salt. Make this up into a loaf and let it rise. Make it about 9 A.M. if you desire the rolls at 6 P.M. At 3 P.M. roll out about half an inch thick; cut in diamonds; butter each one, and, commencing at the corners, roll them up. Put into a flat pan close together and let rise very light. Will bake in half an hour if oven is right.

16. BROILING STEAKS AND CHOPS.

The only way to make a beefsteak delicious is to broil it, and the only way to get the full benefit of it is to take pains in broiling. The first requisite is a perfect broiler ; second, a good clear fire, either wood or coal; third, a good steak. My way of broiling a steak is as follows: I use a cast iron broiler, circular in form, convex, with radiators three quarters of an inch in height, at regular intervals, with a raised opening at the top of the

cone; a fluted gutter passes around the broiler to
receive the drip.   Now comes the secret.   There is
a tin cover deep enough to not touch the steak,
with four half-inch holes in the top and a wooden
knob in the centre to handle it with.   Now for the
steak.   It should be just what one can afford and
never be less than one inch in thickness.   I remove
the bone and the thin skin from the outside of the
fat, and make little incisions to prevent curling.
If for four people, with different tastes, I cut in
four equal parts; now, with a small piece of suet,
grease the tops of the radiators, lay the steak on in
its original shape, now place the cover on carefully, remove the stove lid, place the broiler over
the opening, and proceed to broil to suit the taste
of each, by raising the cover.   I can govern the
broiling, as a portion can be removed at any time.
By this way all the rich juices of the meat are re-
tained.   The dish to receive the broiled steak
should be hot and covered, no salt should be used
until the steak is removed from the broiler, then a
liberal amount of butter should be spread on (not
previously melted, as heat has a tendency to make
it rancid), and salt to taste and serve hot.   The
art once acquired you will never eat a steak broiled
any other way.

17. BROILED TRIPE.

Cut the tripe in small strips; lay in a large wire
broiler and cook gently over a moderate fire until
well browned, turning but once, when it is nearly

done; lay it upon a hot plate; give it a good buttering, season with salt and pepper, and serve.

18. LAMB CHOPS.

Lamb will not keep long after it is killed. Beware of it when the veins, particularly the large vein in the neck, is greenish colored. Lamb is usually considered tender, simply because it is lamb; yet if eaten too soon after killing, it will be very tough. Lamb, like all young meats, should be thoroughly done, and should not be given to invalids, while a mutton chop will be very nutritious and good for them.

The leg will give the larger chops, but the short ribs furnish the daintier ones. See that the butcher cuts them of uniform thickness and trims off all superfluous fat and skin. Wipe off with a damp cloth, scrape the bone clean, take a broad bladed knife and " pat" them flat. Rub the concave bars of the broiler with a little butter or fat, and heat slightly before putting on the chops. Season the chops with pepper and salt, dip in melted butter, then roll in fine bread crumbs; put on the broiler over a fire that is not too bright, as the bread crumbs are easily set on fire. Eight minutes should cook them, with watching.

19. BROILING A STEAK.

One of the most neglected and least understood of the duties of the kitchen is the broiling of a steak. The veriest greenhorn, newly landed, will

tell you she "kin fry a shtake aiqual ter inny wan."
(Deliver me from the fried steak girl!) But it is a
fact that not one in fifty of the so called cooks
know how to cook a steak; and yet there is scarcely
any article of food so universally eaten—by the
hurried man of business and by the epicure, whose
"sauce to (his) meat is ceremony."

There is an old recipe for hare soup, which says:
First catch your hare; quite as important as it is
to say: First catch your steak.

If we could think of the beef as standing and
moving, we could gain a much clearer idea of
which parts were most tender, which most juicy
and nutritious. For they are not generally found
in the same piece. The parts containing the mus-
cles most used in moving are the most juicy and
nutritious, but very tough, while the tender parts
contains very little nutriment.

The porterhouse is the one generally preferred,
but it is not an economical steak. It has a delicious morsel—not the tenderloin—in about the
middle. The sirloin is most generally used, as it
contains more lean and less fat and bone, and
being less expensive is more used for the family.
The round and rump steaks are usually very lean
and tough. Supposing you have purchased a tough
steak, you can make it more tender by placing it
for three hours in a mixture of salad oil and vinegar, in the proportion of three tablespoonfuls of
the former to one of the latter.

Beef should not be too fresh, or almost any part
of it will be tough. It is important to remember

also, that steak will not be tender unless cut across the grain. There is a part on the top of the loin, the fiber of which runs in a different direction from the rest of the loin. As steaks are usually cut, this is very juicy, but tough.. If this could be cut off separately, and then cut across the grain, it makes the finest, juiciest, tenderest and most nutritious steaks in the whole animal.

Inferior beef has hard, skinny fat and dark red lean. Prime beef has bright red lean, and, when pressed by the finger, rises up quickly.

The steak should be evenly cut, about three fourths of an inch thick. If cut any thicker it is apt to be brown on the outside while still uncooked inside. Do not wash the steak. Take a wet cloth and wipe, or rather mop it, but do not pour water on it, and do not lay it in water. Whatever cooks may urge in favor of "pounding" a steak it is not a good thing; it breaks the cells of the meat in which the gravy is contained. If there is a tough piece on the steak it may be "hacked" a little with the back of a kitchen knife, taking care not to break the cells of the meat.

The best broiler is one having concave sides, so as to catch the gravy and prevent the fat from catching fire and smoking. Heat the broiler, then wipe with a clean cloth; just before using rub the bars with suet, to prevent them from marking the meat. A clear, brisk fire is necessary, but not too close to the steak; throw a little salt on the fire, place your broiler over until the bars are heated through, then put on your steak and watch con-

stantly to keep it from smoking, burning, or catching fire, lifting it up when necessary, but not turning until the one side is nicely browned; then turn
to the other side and brown that; turn once more,
that is, twice for each side. The object is to cook
the outside as quickly as possible, so as to keep in
all the juices of the meat. Just before lifting from
the fire shake pepper and salt lightly over. Have
the platter hot, dot it with specks of butter.

A very little carelessness will ruin all your pre-
vious care; a charred bone, a black burned spot, or
an underdone one will spoil the effect on both eyes
and appetite.

With the right kind of a fire, and an evenly cut
steak, seven minutes is enough to allow for the
broiling generally. This should make it evenly
browned outside, and a rich juicy red within.
Place the steak on the platter, dot the top with
butter, and serve hot as possible. My word for it,
the game will be well worth the candle.

20. "POUPIC" CUTLETS.

Fry to a nice brown one half dozen slices of sugar cured bacon. Remove to a warm platter, add
a piece of butter to the bacon fat in pan, and place
same number of veal cutlets neatly trimmed, dipped
in egg, bread crumbs and finely chopped parsley.
When done place on dish with slices of bacon alternate and thin slices of lemon on each cutlet.
For gravy stew the veal trimmings, adding salt,
pepper, teaspoon of walnut catsup, and squeeze of

lemon juice, thicken with flour and butter and pour over cutlets.

21. VEAL CUTLETS—BREADED.

Have the butcher cut two pounds of cutlets in pieces about four inches square, and scarify well on one side. Salt and pepper to taste. Roll fine five soda crackers. Beat well two eggs, into which dip each piece of meat and then into the pulverized cracker. Fry slowly in plenty of hot lard until well browned. When done remove from pan and put about one half teacupful of water in the pan, bring to a boil and pour over the meat.

ROASTING AND BOILING MEATS.

22. HOW TO PREPARE ROAST BEEF.

Take about eight pounds of porterhouse roast, have your butcher remove the bone and nearly all the fat around the tenderloin or fillet, and then tie it and fasten with skewers into a circular shape. Lard it with the fatty part of bacon cut in thin strips. Place in your roasting pan with two onions cut in quarters, inserting a clove into each quarter; add a bay leaf.

Sprinkle your meat well on all sides with salt and pepper, a little thyme, and dredge well with flour; add from two to three cupfuls of stock, as it makes your gravy richer than using water alone.

Place in a well-heated oven and baste as often as

possible to keep the meat juicy; when well browned on top turn bottom side up and brown that also all around.

Allow about two hours for this piece. It will be nicely browned and still rare at the heart. When done place it on a heated platter and turn into a warming oven. Now prepare the gravy. Remove all the fat from the contents of the pan. Mix in a cup a spoonful of flour, with cold water, until smooth. Add to your contents of pan. Place on the stove. Add a little salt, and allow to boil until smooth and quite a little thick, stirring constantly. It can then be strained or not, as desired. Pour into gravy dish and serve with the meat.

23. ROAST BEEF.

Place an old-fashioned iron spider on top of the stove, and, when smoking hot, put in the roast, which has previously been thoroughly rubbed with a damp cloth. Sear one side and turn it over. Salt, pepper, and dredge with flour the seared side. By this time it will be ready to turn again. Treat this side in the same manner. It is now ready to roast, and if you choose, can be roasted in the same spider. Allow fifteen minutes to the pound. It is always an improvement to set a basin of water in the oven while roasting meat. The merits of this plan of preparing beef over that of the old are obvious. Searing the meat quickly on both sides prevents the escape of the juices, making the meat more juicy, nutritious, and palatable.

24. BAKED HAM

Very few know how delicate and sweet a ham can taste unless they have eaten it properly baked. They generally class it in their minds with ham sandwiches or ham and eggs, and know nothing of it in any other forms than these. Take a large sweet ham, soak it for two hours in cold water, then dry and scrape all the smoke-browned parts and wipe it off with a damp cloth. Put on in cold water and allow it to come quickly to a boil. Then set it back on the range, where it will only simmer. Let it boil (very slowly) for two hours; take from the fire and allow it to partly cool in the water. Place in a baking pan, sprinkle well with flour, and baste frequently with a half pint of good sweet cider. Cook for one hour longer. Then take it from the oven, slip a pointed knife under the skin and remove it entire, also the flour crust, turn out all of the dripping in the pan. Shake powdered sugar over the ham until well covered and return to the oven to brown. It is ready for the table, and a gravy made of half a pint of fresh cider (that with which it was basted is too brown), a tablespoonful of the ham drippings, a teaspoonful of sugar, just allow the gravy to heat. Served in a sauce boat. To be extremely delicious pour two glasses of champagne over before covering with sugar. Some may not like the sweet taste of the sugar. If so, cover with grated bread crumbs and place in the oven; or a delicious champagne sauce is made by this recipe. Mix thoroughly a table-

spoonful of butter with one of flour. Set on the
fire and stir until a rosy brown, add half a pint of
hot strong beef stock. Stir slowly, and after the
sauce has boiled up once, season well with pepper
and salt, and strain; then add half a cupful of
champagne or wine. If your principles or pocket do
not object, you will be satisfied. The ham is as
good cold as hot.

25. ROASTING MEAT.

Be careful in selecting to get meat that has a
bright color. The fat should be clear and firm.
Good meat is generally large and fat. Lean meat
may have less fat to the pound, but it will not be
so juicy and tender. A cut from the ribs makes a
good prime roasting piece. Have the butcher dress
it. Be sure he gives you a piece of suet with it.
To prepare the meat for the oven remove all blem-
ishes by wiping with a damp cloth or scraping with
a knife. Do not wash your meat. Make a few
cuts on the outside to keep it from bulging in the
middle. Sprinkle with pepper. Cut the suet in
small pieces and lay it on the top. Have the
oven at its highest temperature when the meat is
ready. A warm oven will extract the juice and
make a rich gravy, but at the risk of spoiling
the meat. A hot oven hardens the albumen on
the outside, forming a covering which retains
the richness. With this covering the meat will
cook in its own liquor, making the roast sweet
and juicy when served. Allow fifteen minutes'

roasting to each pound of weight. When in the oven a half hour sprinkle with salt; cool the oven a little to keep from burning. A few minutes afterward commence basting with the drippings in the pan; baste three or four times at intervals. When it is done remove the suet, put a fork through the fat part of the meat and remove from the pan to the platter. Put it in oven to keep warm while you are making the gravy. To make the gravy take two teaspoonfuls of flour; put in a cup, mix with a little water, enough to make a thick paste; beat smooth and add more water. Prepare this just after the meat is put in the oven, then the starch in the flour will have time to soak, making the work easier. Place the pan on the back of the stove and put in most of the flour and water; pour in boiling water; keep stirring until all are thoroughly mixed. Move the pan to the front of stove until it boils for a minute. This will make a good gravy to serve with potatoes. When the carving is done a rich gravy of meat juice will follow the knife and settle in the dish, which can be served with the meat.

26. ROAST HAM, WINE SAUCE, TENNESSEE STYLE.

Take a country ham from 10 to 12 pounds weight, soak over night in tepid water, then wash, scrape, and trim off all rusty fat, cut off the knuckle bone, rinse in very cold water, and put into a pot deep enough to cover it entirely; boil gently five

to six hours, then take up, drain, and skin ; with a
sharp, short knife cut through the under side to the
bone; take it out and fill its place with a stuffing
made of half pint of flour, half pint of corn meal,
pinch of salt, the same of black pepper and red
pepper, two eggs, tablespoonful powdered sage,
one small minced onion, and cream enough to make
a stiff batter. Fry in sweet lard, stirring all the
time. When the ham is stuffed skewer it together
and let drip for an hour ; then put it into a clean,
deep pan, score the fat in crossway slices, pour
over it a quart bottle of good red wine, then sprinkle with sugar and black and red pepper, and set
in a warm, not hot, oven for two hours. Serve
cold in the thinnest possible slices, cut all the way
through. If properly prepared the wine will all be
absorbed and give its flavor to every shred of meat.

27. SADDLE OF VENISON.

This is the best cut of venison and should always
be roasted either before the open fire or in a hot
oven. Lard the meat well with fat pork or bacon
and sprinkle with salt. Place in a baking pan with
a cup of water and two ounces of butter, baste
often enough so that the meat shall not once become dry. Bake one hour for every three pounds.
Prepare the gravy in the roasting pan as for other
baked and roasted meat. Add three or four tablespoonfuls of currant jelly to the gravy, and put a
mold of currant jelly on the table to be served with
the vension.

28. ROAST TURKEY.

In choosing the bird one can readily tell whether it is young or not. If the lower end of the breast bone is soft and bends easily, the breast plump and fat white, rest assured it is young. It is necessary to know this to determine the length of time required in cooking. When old or very large and fat the flavor is apt to be strong. This method of cooking, however, removes this unpleasant savor. No matter how old the bird it will be tender, moist, sweet, and delicious, to say nothing of being more digestible than when cooked in the ordinary manner.

First singe over blazing paper. With a sharp knife remove the pin feathers. If not already drawn at the butcher's, open the vent and draw out the internal organs, taking care not to break the gall. Pull out the windpipe from the neck. Wash outside, being careful not to break the skin if tender. Turn back the skin and cut the neck short, and with a large needle and thread fasten the skin neatly over it with two or three stitches. Then proceed to fill with the following forcemeat:

Take stale bread (the quantity depends on the size of the turkey), grate fine into a dish, add pepper, salt, a generous portion of butter, and sufficient sage that has been pulverized by passing through a sieve, to give it the proper flavor. A few raw oysters may be added, if desired. Pour over the whole a small quantity of water, say a gill for stuffing for a small turkey, cover with another dish and let steam for fifteen minutes, then remove the cover and stir lightly to thoroughly mix the ingredients. Do not fill the turkey too full, as the filling is apt to swell a little in cooking. Close the opening made in drawing with needle and thread. With a skewer fasten the legs together, run the skewer into the bone of the tail and tie securely. Run another skewer through the two wings, fastening them to the sides of the bird. Place in a steamer (a tall one may be procured for the purpose with a ring in the top to fasten to, and movable trays that can be used for a variety of things) ; half fill the pan below with water, renewing when necessary, and throw in the giblets. To clean these, separate the liver from the gall with a sharp knife. Cut lightly around the gizzard and pull it gently apart, peeling out the contents without breaking the inner skin, if possible. Let the turkey steam for two hours, or until done, which may be ascertained by trying the breast with a fork. If done there, it is cooked through. A small bird may require less time and a very tough one more. When done, transfer to a baking tin. Pour a sufficient quantity of the water over which it was steamed into the baking tin to use in basting while baking. Upon examination the skin will be found covered with blisters. Prick each one with a fork; then rub butter over every part of the turkey. Place in the oven and bake brown, basting frequently. One half hour is required to brown properly unless it has been prepared for the oven the day before (as it may be), when additional time will be necessary to heat

through. Before serving cut the strings and remove and draw out the skewers. Serve with cran-
berry sauce.

29. HOW TO BOIL BEEF.

Take about four to five pounds of rump beef
or cross rib (the first cut). Ask your butcher to
lard the same with small pieces of salt bacon. All
butchers do this willingly, and it will save you an
amount of trouble. Then take about half of a carrot, cut it into tiny pieces; also take an ordinary
sized pickle, and if you have a few slices of pickled
beets, cut them and the pickle in the same manner
as you did the carrot. With the meat fork make
little holes all over the beef, then fill the holes with
the pieces, alternating from one to another—carrot, pickle, beef, carrot, pickle, beef, etc. The beau-
tiful appearance of this beef, when sliced, depends
entirely upon the above being done with care and
taste. You then cut two onions into slices, place a
plate into the bottom of the sauccpan in which the
beef is to be cooked. Put the onions on the plate,
cut from the rump some of the fat, and chop same
into very small pieces, and add this to the onions;
also one laurel leaf and a few whole allspice and
pepper. Now put sufficient pepper and salt on the
beef, then roll it in flour, being careful to cover it
with same on all sides. Now put the meat upon
the onions and pour boiling water over it, so that it
is covered to about three quarters of its size. Close
it with a well-fitting cover, and let it boil slowly but

uninterruptedly for from three to three and a half hours. By adding a few of either fresh or canned tomatoes a half an hour before you wish to serve the beef it improves greatly the flavor of the gravy. The gravy should be run through a colander before sending it to the table. This beef is excellent when cold for either lunch or tea.

30. BOILED CORNED BEEF.

Select the juicy cuts which are sold at 7 cents a pound, as such meat has the best flavor. Put the beef in cold water for two hours. Pour off the water. Put in cold water enough to cover it. Bring it up to boiling and pour off again. Add again enough cold water to cover. Bring it to a boil and let it simmer three hours, skimming off the grease. The meat may be served hot or sliced when cold.

31. PORK CAKE.

Chop fine one pound fat salt pork free from lean or rind, so as to be almost like lard, and pour over it one half pint boiling water, two cups of sugar, one and a half cups of molasses, two eggs, one teaspoon of soda rubbed fine and dissolved in the molasses; nutmeg and cloves, of each one tablespoon; cinnamon two tablespoons, raisins chopped fine one pound, currants one half pound, citron quarter pound, sliced thin. Add flour enough to make it the consistency of common soft molasses cake. Bake slow and try with broom splint to tell when done. This recipe will make two loaves.

32. BAKED MUTTON.

Take a leg of mutton weighing six or eight pounds, cut down the under side and remove the bone; fill with dressing made of four ounces of suet, eight ounces of stale bread, two beaten eggs, one onion, a little thyme, salt and pepper. Sew up; cook in a pan in a hot oven about three hours. Baste with butter. Thicken the gravy with browned flour and serve with pickles.

33 VEAL PATE.

Two pounds of nice finely chopped fresh veal, one beaten egg poured into the veal and well mixed. Then soak half a dozen ordinary soda crackers in hot water till thoroughly softened, and add these. Mix all carefully. Put to this a scant half cupful of milk. Season very highly with salt and pepper. Pile up in loaf form in a moderate sized tin. Bake a little over one hour. This is a very palatable tea dish.

34. VEAL POTPOURRI.

Boil till tender the liver and heart of a calf, with two or three veal tongues. Chop very fine, and season with salt, pepper, and butter, adding vinegar to taste. This is good hot, or put up in small jars comes in nicely as a royal relish at cold collations, picnics, etc.

35. SWEETBREADS.

Veal sweetbreads are the best. Get them fresh
as they spoil very soon; wash them and remove
any skin or pipes that may adhere. Put to soak for
two or three hours in cold, slightly salted water;
then parboil twenty minutes, or until tender. Throw
into cold water for ten minutes to whiten them and
set in a cool place. When ready to cook them, dip
into beaten egg, then into cracker dust, and fry in
hot butter or beef drippings.

36. FRICANDEAU OF VEAL.

Take a four pound fillet of veal, trim to a nice
shape, and lard on top. Put thin slices of pork in
a saucepan, lay over the pork sliced carrot, a stalk
of celery, some parsley and an onion. Put the
meat on top of the vegetables, sprinkle over pepper
and salt. Fill the saucepan with boiling stock to
cover the meat. Cover with light lid and bake in
moderate oven two hours and a half. Baste several times.

37. HARICOT.

Fry an onion; then cut all the fat from the chops;
flour them well and brown them in the onion; cover
with water and stew slowly for two or three hours;
then add tomato, cucumber, or any other vegetables,
or cover with a can of tomatoes instead of the
water.

38. SMOKED BEEF AND EGGS.

Beat six eggs together, pour into a well buttered skillet, and add immediately one quarter of a pound of smoked beef, cut fine. Stir until the eggs are mixed through the beef and are cooked done.

39. ENGLISH BEEFSTEAK PUDDING.

Five pounds of best sirloin steak. Remove bones and cut in pieces of right size to serve on table.

Have a three-quart earthen bowl. Wet a medium coarse muslin, three quarters of a yard in size, in water, and spread smoothly in the bowl.

Sift four quarts of flour in another bowl. Chop and pick until white and creamy one pound of best suet. Put it in the flour with half a teaspoon of salt, and mix thoroughly.

Wet with warm milk and water until it can be easily rolled. Cut off one pound of the dough, and roll the rest large enough to line the bowl next to the cloth. Put in a layer of meat. Season with salt and pepper. Repeat this until the meat is all in.

Take a tablespoonful of flour, and mix fine in a coffee cup of lukewarm water, and add to the meat.

Draw the edges of crust toward the meat, and dampen well the edges with water; roll out the one pound of dough left, and fit in the top, and pinch well together until there is no fear of leakage. Take up the cloth, adjusting the fullness evenly, and tie with a strong string one inch above the pudding to make room for light crust. Drop and cover in a china lined kettle of boiling water and boil without cessation for five hours, keeping the pudding covered with boiling water. When done and ready to serve, take into a large pan, untie the string, remove the cloth carefully, lest the crust be broken; place on a large, deep platter, already garnished with parsley; cut from the top a circular piece of crust large enough to remove the meat and gravy as needed, cutting the remainder of the crust around the entire pudding, so as to keep the bottom whole to save loss of gravy, which is delicious, and also to warm if any is left over.

40. SPICED BEEF.

Get about three pounds of beef, the round, and boil until very tender. Then take out of the water, chop fine; and season to taste. Put in a tablespoonful each of ground cloves, allspice, and cinnamon. Mix well and pack in a square tin. Take the water it has been boiled in, and let it boil down to about two thirds of a cupful, salt and pepper a little, and pour over the meat. Let it get cold.

41. CHICKEN FRICASSEE.

Cut and clean the chicken, and scald and skin it completely. With a sharp knife remove all the meat from the bones. The bones, with the neck and feet, can be used for a most delicious clear chicken soup. Place the chicken meat in a stew pan with one onion cut into six pieces, a few sprigs of chopped parsley, a little salt and pepper, and a

few drops of lemon juice. Put in a piece of butter
as large as an egg, and a pint of water. Cover
close and stew for one hour. Then lift and strain
off the gravy, into which beat gradually a cup of
cream and the yelks of two eggs. Set this gravy
into a dish of boiling water until it is quite hot,
but do not let it boil. Then flour over the fricas-
see.

42. CHICKEN PIE.

Singe and unjoint two young and tender chickens.
Wash quickly and lightly to keep sweetness in the
fowl. Divide backbone and breast, and put in
kettle with quart of water. Season with salt and
pepper. Steam until slightly tender, make a crust
like biscuit, only shorter; do not knead it. Stir
baking powder through flour; add salt, shortening,
and milk or water, stirring lightly with a spoon
until you have soft dough. Flour the kneading
board and lightly roll crust half an inch thick.
Line a deep baking-pan, put in a layer of chicken,
dust with flour and add little lumps of butter.
After all the chicken is in the pan, pour over it
some of the broth and dust with a little flour,
pepper, and salt. Put on top crust ; prick holes
for steam to escape. A nice way for any pie is to
cut a hole in center of crust. Make a tunnel of
stiff paper by wrapping around the finger. Let it
stand upright in center of pie, and the juice will
boil up in the tunnel instead of over the pie. Bake
until crust is done and lightly brown.

43. CHICKEN CROQUETTES.

Boil a large tender chicken. Season with salt
and pepper. When cooked cut the chicken into
small pieces. Mince the half of a small onion with
two sprigs of parsley. Put one ounce of butter in
a saucepan. When hot put in the onion and parsley,
with half a teacup of flour. Stew until a light
brown, then pour over a teacup of soup stock and
stir until a smooth paste is formed; add salt,
pepper, a little grated nutmeg, and the juice of a
small lemon. Mix well and put in the chicken.
Mold into croquette shape and fry in boiling lard.

44. JELLIED CHICKEN.

One good-sized chicken, boiled until very tender,
season with salt and pepper while boiling; let the
liquor cool, skim off the oil: heat it again and stir
in one tablespoonful of gelatine which has been
soaked one hour in two tablespoonfuls of water;
slice two hard-boiled eggs very thin, placing around
the sides and on the bottom of dish; cut the
chicken quite fine with a knife, leaving out the skin;
place it lightly in the dish with the eggs, pour
the liquor over it; have only enough to cover.
When hardened turn out on a platter garnished
with celery tops or parsley. Nice tea dish.

45. VENISON PASTY.

The neck, breast, and shoulder are the parts
used for a venison pie or pasty. Cut the meat

into pieces (fat and lean together) and put the
bones and trimmings into a stew-pan with pepper,
salt, and water, or veal broth enough to cover it.
Simmer it till you have drawn out a good gravy,
then strain it.   In the meantime make a good rich
paste and roll it rather thick.   Cover the sides and
bottom of a deep dish with one sheet of it and put
in your meat, having seasoned it with pepper and
salt, nutmeg and mace.   Pour in the gravy which
you have prepared from the trimmings and two
glasses of port or claret, and lay on the top some
bits of butter rolled in flour.   Cover the pie with
a lid of paste ornamented with paste leaves.   Bake
two hours or more according to size.

COOKING VEGETABLES.

46. BAKED STUFFED TOMATOES.

Take ripe, firm tomatoes, cut a small piece off
the top, and then cut out the inside, leaving enough
to make a firm cup to hold the stuffing.   Chop the
inside with bread crumbs and an onion, season with
pepper and salt, and put into the tomato.   Put a
small piece of butter on each tomato.   Bake in a
pan until they are lightly browned on top.   I generally take one onion to six tomatoes.   The exact
amount of bread crumbs depends upon the size of
the tomatoes, as some are more juicy than others.

47. POTATO CAKE.

Peel and boil in salted water six or eight large potatoes. When quite tender drain and mash fine. Sprinkle the bread with flour, turn the potatoes on it, add more flour and work together until a rather stiff dough is formed. Then roll out with rolling-pin about three quarters of an inch thick. Cut in squares or cut with biscuit cutter. Have the griddle hot, dip each piece in flour and bake to a light brown on both sides. Remove to a warm platter, spread lightly with butter, and serve at once.

48. POTATO CROQUETTES.

Season cold mashed potatoes with pepper and salt, and beat them to a cream. To every cupful of potatoes add a tablespoonful of melted butter; also add two or three beaten eggs and some minced parsley. Roll into small balls. Fry in hot lard.

49. POTATO PUFF.

Take two cupfuls of cold mashed potato and stir into two tablespoonfuls of melted butter, beating to a white cream before adding anything else. Then put with this two eggs, whipped very light, and a teacupful of cream or milk, salting to taste. Beat all well, pour in a deep dish, and bake in a quick oven until it is nicely browned. If properly mixed it will come out of the oven light, puffy, and nice.

50. POTATO SALAD.

Slice some large, cold, boiled potatoes very thin and place them in a salad dish, or arrange them in a pyramid and pour the following mixture over them: Boil an egg very hard, mash the yelk, add one raw yelk, one teaspoonful of cornstarch, one of vinegar, one of best salad oil, one half teaspoonful of mixed mustard, one of salt, one half spoon of cayenne pepper, two of butter, and beat all thoroughly together. Ornament with slices of boiled eggs, parsley, or sliced lemons.

51. BAKED TURNIPS.

Pare four good-sized turnips ; cut in thick slices; cook until tender in salted water ; drain and lay in a baking dish. Make a sauce as follows: Two large tablespoonfuls of flour, two of butter ; stir these together in frying-pan ; when thoroughly heated and mixed add a teacup of milk, pouring in gradually; add very little salt and pepper and bits of butter over top of turnips; pour the sauce over and bake in a brisk oven twenty minutes.

52. SUCCOTASH.

Take eight to twelve ears of young sweet corn, according to size; cut off the corn, lengthwise of the ear, and not cutting deep; put it in your kettle with three quarts of cold water, boil half an hour, skim and add one quart of shelled green Lima beans; boil one hour and then scrape the milk from

the cobs with the back of a silver knife, mix with
the beans and corn, take from the fire and let it
stand on top of stove for a few minutes, then pour
all into a large dish and season with pepper and
salt to taste, adding one cup of sweet butter.

53. CAULIFLOWER.

Place a head of cauliflower in salt water for a
few minutes to remove insects. Boil twenty minutes in salt water, drain on sieve, and put it in a
buttered dish. Melt a piece of butter the size of
an egg, add to it one tablespoonful of flour, stir on
the fire one minute, and add a gill of milk, and pepper and salt. Stir this sauce until it boils. Pour
over the cauliflower, sprinkle over it a few browned
bread crumbs, and set it in a moderate oven for a
few minutes to bake.

54. ASPARAGUS.

Have the stalks of equal length and scrape the
white part of the stalks from the asparagus. Then
place in cold water for a time before using. Tie in
bunches, place in a stewpan containing about half
a gallon of water, and a tablespoonful of salt.
Boil quickly from twenty to thirty minutes. Have
some thin slices of toasted bread on hot dish; drain
the asparagus and arrange on the toast. Serve
while hot, with butter.

55. BOILED ASPARAGUS.

Cut off the tough ends, put in boiling water, which has salt in it, and cook until tender. For a bunch of asparagus, make a sauce of a pint of milk, a tablespoon of butter, pepper and salt to taste, and a heaping tablespoon of flour; have ready a few slices of toasted bread, on which lay the asparagus, well drained; pour over all the boiling sauce and serve.

56. DELICIOUS CABBAGE.

Slice or chop fine a small head of cabbage, salt and pepper, and cook in just enough water to keep from burning; take half a cup sour cream, half a cup vinegar, two eggs, butter size of an egg; beat together, pour over the cabbage; let it boil and serve at once.

57. CABBAGE BALLS.

Cold mutton, lamb, or veal. Take one half dozen nice cabbage leaves; wilt in warm water; one and a half pounds of meat; two tablespoonfuls of boiled rice or cold bread dressing, one small onion; meat and onion chopped fine; one pinch of salt and pepper; half teaspoon thyme; mix all together; add a spoonful of butter; make into six balls; tie each in a cabbage leaf; boil in a large bottomed pot, and a quart of water, and any gravy you have on hand; boil one half hour over a slow fire; serve in leaves, with gravy.

58. STEAMED CABBAGE.

Chop cabbage fine; take tablespoonful of butter, put in pan and brown; put in this half a cup of vinegar, and half a cup ef white sugar. Let this come to a boil; then add previously beaten one egg, half cup of cream, half teaspoonful of corn-starch; stir these in the boiling vinegar. Pour this dressing boiling hot over cabbage and cover close, and let it stand on back of range a little time before serving.

59. CABBAGE SALAD.

Half pint vinegar, pinch of salt, two thirds of a cup of sugar; set to simmer. Take half a cup of cream, one egg well beaten, one teaspoonful of cornstarch, one teaspoonful of mustard, ground. Stir these well together and stir into the boiling vinegar; boil a minute, stirring constantly one way. Mix this thoroughly with chopped cabbage.

60. BAKED TOMATOES.

Get them as large and sound as possible. Cut off the upper half, remove the seed and fill with cracker crumbs; put a small piece of butter on top of the cracker. Place on the upper half of the tomato and bake twenty minutes in hot oven. Be careful not to have them burn or become dry.

61. TOMATO SOUP.

To one quart of stewed tomatoes, strained, that no seeds remain, add a generous quart of boiling milk. Put a pinch of butter the size of an egg in the tureen, and add two tablespoonfuls of rolled cracker, and salt and pepper to taste. Pour over this the boiling milk, then add the strained tomatoes; mix thoroughly.

62. TOMATO CATSUP.

Boil your tomatoes and strain through a sieve. To one gallon of tomatoes add one quart vinegar, four teaspoonfuls salt, four whole black peppers, four spoonfuls mustard, four spoonfuls white sugar, one ounce bruised ginger, one small teaspoonful red pepper (or two bell peppers boiled with the tomatoes), four onions, a small handful of fresh peach leaves. Boil all for three hours on a slow fire. If peach leaves cannot be had, use two tablespoonfuls bruised peach pits. Tie all the seasoning in a thin muslin bag.

63. BAKED MACARONI.

Break the macaroni in pieces about an inch long. Boil in hot salted water twenty minutes. Have ready a dish of grated cheese, and a greased baking-dish. When macaroni is soft, place alternate layers of macaroni and cheese till all is used, having cheese for top layer. Then sprinkle salt, pepper, and bits of butter on top, and pour on milk enough to be seen when dish is tipped. Bake twenty minutes or half an hour.

64. INDIAN PUDDING.

One quart milk, two heaping tablespoonfuls of Indian meal, four of sugar, one of butter, three eggs, one teaspoon of salt and half teaspoon ginger. Boil the milk, stirring the meal into it, and cook about twelve minutes; stir the butter into the meal and milk, and when cool add the beaten eggs, salt, sugar and ginger. Bake slowly one hour.

65. LETTUCE SALAD.

Use the crisp leaves, cold and fresh, without cutting, and dress with mayonnaise sauce flavored with fresh lemon-juice. This is the best of all salads.

66. CRANBERRY SAUCE.

Wash the berries in cold water after picking out all soft or defective ones. Put into scalding water two minutes; then drain, and to every pound of berries add a half pint of cold water. Place the kettle into another kettle of boiling water; cover close and do not stir the berries. When they have boiled five minutes add a half pound of granulated sugar for each pound of fruit and let boil two minutes longer. By this means the fruit will be whole and of a bright color. Always serve the berries with their juice, otherwise the sauce is too dry and bitter,

67. VEGETABLE SALAD.

Take the four sliced potatoes, two carrots, and two turnips which have been cooked in the corned beef soup, chop and mix two cups of cabbage and two of celery and arrange in alternate layers with the cooked vegetables in a salad dish, adding mayonnaise dressing flavored with fresh lemon-juice.

MAKING PASTRY.

68. WHITE LAYER CAKE.

One cup sugar, one half cup butter, one half cup sweet milk, two cups flour, one and a half teaspoonfuls baking powder, whites of four eggs. Sift the baking powder through the flour two or three times. Whip the eggs to a stiff froth. Cream the butter and sugar, add half the milk and flour, beating thoroughly; add remainder, and last of all beat in the eggs. The yelks can be used in the same way for golden cake. Bake in layer tins, and when cold spread with any one of the following fillings :

FILLINGS FOR CAKE.

Caramel.—Two cups sugar, one half cup cream, one piece of butter the size of a walnut. Cook until it candies in water, stirring all the time; then beat until cold and add one half teaspoonful of vanilla.

Maple Sugar.—Two cups maple sugar cooked until it strings. Add beaten whites of two eggs and beat until cold.

Apple.—One and a half cups sugar, juice and grated rind of one lemon, two grated apples, whites of two eggs ; all beaten thoroughly together.

Chocolate.—Whites of three eggs, one and a half cups sugar, three tablespoonfuls chocolate, one teaspoonful vanilla.

Chocolate Icing.—Small pieces of chocolate grated, one cup sugar, white of one egg; well beaten.

Orange Icing.—Rind and piece of one orange and lemon, one cup of sugar, white of egg well beaten.

Boiled Frosting.—Six tablespoonfuls of sugar to the white of one egg. Water enough to dissolve the sugar, and boil until it waxes. Add the waxed sugar to the beaten egg while hot and beat until cool. Beat into this desiccated cocoanut for cocoanut filling.

Pineapple.—One and a half cups of sugar, two pieces of candied pineapple chopped in small pieces, or half a can of grated pineapple without the juice. Boil until it waxes. Add the beaten whites of two eggs and beat until cold. This last filling is particularly delicate.

All boiled frostings should be added to the whites of the eggs while hot, and beaten constantly until cold enough to spread.

69. FRENCH PUFF PASTE.

Take equal quantities of flour and butter, say one pound of each, half a saltspoonful of salt, the white of one egg, and rather more than one fourth of a pint of water. Weigh the flour, ascertain that it is perfectly dry, and sift it; squeeze all the water from the butter, and wring it in a clean cloth till there is no moisture remaining. Put the flour into a large bowl, and work lightly into it one quarter of the butter; into this put the white of the egg, well beaten, the salt and about one fourth of a pint of ice cold water (the quantity of water must be regulated by the cook, as it is impossible to give the exact proportion of it), knead up the paste quickly and lightly, and, when smooth, roll it out square to the thickness of about half an inch. Presuming that the butter is perfectly free from moisture and as cool as possible, roll it into a ball and place this ball on the center of the paste; fold the paste over the butter all around, and secure it by wrapping it well all over. Flatten the paste by rolling it lightly with the rolling-pin until it is quite thin, but not thin enough to allow the butter to break through, and keep the board and paste dredged lightly with flour during the process of making. This rolling gives it the first turn. Now fold the paste in three thicknesses and roll out again, and should the weather be very warm put it in a cool place or on ice to cool between the several turns. Unless kept cool the paste will be spoiled. Roll out the paste twice, put it by to cool, then roll it out three times more, which will make seven turnings in all. Now fold paste in two and set in a cold place or on the ice until ready to use. If well made and properly baked this crust will be delicious and should rise in the oven very much. The paste should be made rather firm in the first instance, as the butter is liable to break through. You must also avoid getting it too soft. Great attention must be paid to keeping the butter cool. When covering baking dishes with puff paste handle the paste as deftly and lightly as possible if you would have light crust. Cut the paste from the edge of the baking dish with a sharp knife, first dipped in hot water or flour.

70. ENGLISH WALNUT CAKE.

One cup of sugar, one half cup of butter, one half cup of milk, two cups of flour, two eggs, one heaping teaspoonful of baking powder, one large cup of stoned raisins, one large cup of chopped walnuts. Flour the nuts and raisins before putting them in the cake. This is very good and not expensive.

71. RIBBON CAKE.

Take one and a quarter cups sugar, one half cup butter, one half cup sweet milk, three eggs, and two teaspoonfuls of baking powder; beat thoroughly. Divide in three parts, and to one third add one tablespoonful of molasses, one teaspoonful each of cinnamon, cloves, and nutmeg; bake in three layers, and put the dark between the two white layers, placing sufficient icing or jelly between; ice the top.

72. CREAM PUFFS.

One cup hot water, one half cup butter, boil together, and while boiling stir in one cup of sifted flour, dry. Take from the stove and stir to smooth paste, and after this cools stir in three eggs, not beaten. Stir five minutes. Drop in tablespoon-fuls on a buttered tin and bake in a quick oven twenty-five minutes. Don't let them touch each other in the pan and do not open the oven door oftener than absolutely necessary. For the cream, one cup milk, one half cup sugar, one egg, three tablespoons flour or two cornstarch. Dissolve cornstarch in a little milk. Put the rest of the milk on the stove. When hot stir in the sugar and egg, beaten together, and cornstarch. Cook until thick. Flavor with vanilla. When both this and puffs are cool open one side of the puffs and fill with the cream. This makes one dozen puffs.

72. NEAPOLITAN CAKE.

One cup brown sugar, three eggs, half a cup of butter, half a cup of molasses, half a cup of strong coffee, three cups of flour, one teaspoonful of bak-ing powder, one cup of raisins, and one of currants ; a teaspoonful each of cinnamon, cloves, and mace. Bake in jelly cake pan. For white part take two cups of sugar, one of butter, three of flour, half a cup of milk, a teaspoonful of baking powder and the whites of four eggs. Bake in jelly pans and put together alternately, with icing flavored with vanlila between. Ice the top.

Icing.—Take the whites of two eggs and stir in one pound of powdered sugar. Flavor with vanilla.

73. ANGEL CAKE.

Whites of eleven eggs, one and one half cups of sugar, one cup of flour sifted four times, one teaspoon of cream tartar, one teaspoon of vanilla ; cream tartar sifted in the flour. Beat the whites and stir in the sugar, add extract and stir the flour lightly. Do not grease the tin ; bake forty minutes in a slow oven. The kind of tin to bake it in : Go to the tin shop and get a six-quart pan, have a pipe made in the center which will be two inches in diameter and smaller at the top. When the cake is baked turn the tin upside down and let it be until the cake drops from the tin.

74. FIG CAKE.

Two cups sugar, three cups flour, one cup milk, half cup butter, three eggs, beaten separately, whites added last ; three teaspoonfuls of baking powder ; flavor as you like ; bake in tins, six by ten inches ; three layers.

Filling for Fig Cake.—One pound figs, chopped fine. Add one half cup hot water, scant half cup of sugar, put in a basin, set this into water and boil until smooth ; spread between the layers.

Frosting for the Same.—One pound of powdered sugar, half pint of boiling water ; boil until thick as mucilage or strings from the spoon ; then beat until white ; spread on the cake hot.

75. LOCKPORT CAKE.

Three eggs, two cups sugar, one cup butter, three cups flour, one cup sweet milk, three teaspoonfuls of baking powder ; divide into three parts, take two, add to the third two tablespoonfuls of molasses, one teaspoonful of all kinds of spices, one half cup of flour, one cup chopped raisins ; this is the center layer, to be put together with white frosting or chocolate, the chocolate to be made as follows : One cup sugar, three fourths cup grated chocolate, one half cup water ; let boil until it strings from the spoon or holds together when dropped into water. This cake is best baked in tins six by ten inches.

76. SARATOGA CAKE.

Two eggs well beaten, one and a half cups of sugar, two tablespoonfuls of butter, one cup of milk, one half teaspoonful of lemon extract (vanilla if preferred), two full cups of flour, and two teaspoonfuls of baking powder. For frosting, beat the whites of two eggs to a stiff froth, then add seven tablespoonfuls of powdered sugar and flavor with one half teaspoonful of either lemon or vanilla extract ; when the cake is done, take out of oven

and let it stand fifteen minutes or more before
frosting, after which return it to the oven only long
enough to form a crust without being colored.

77. CREAM SPONGE CAKE.

One coffee-cup of sugar, one coffee-cup of sifted
flour, four eggs, four and one half tablespoons of
milk, two teaspoons of baking powder sifted in
with the flour, a little salt and lemon essence.
Bake in two jelly tins.

Cream Filling.—Pint of thick sweet cream, sweetened and flavored with vanilla. Beat with an egg
beater until very stiff. Spread between and on top
of the layers of sponge cake.

78. A PYRAMID OF TARTS.

Roll out a sufficient quantity of the best puff
paste, and, with oval or circular cutters, cut it out
into seven or eight pieces of different sizes, stamp-
ing the middle of each with the cutter you intend
using for the next. Bake all separately, and when
cool place them on a dish in a pyramid, the largest
piece at the bottom, the smallest at the top. Take
various preserved or fresh fruits and lay some of
the largest on the lower piece of paste; the next
smaller, and so on till you finish at the top with
the smallest fruit you have. The upper bar may
be small enough to hold a single raspberry or
strawberry.

79. CINDERELLAS.

One pint rich milk, one fourth pound melted
butter, four tablespoonfuls sifted flour.   Beat four
eggs very light and stir them gradually into the
milk and butter alternately with the flour.   Add a
half of a small grated nutmeg and a half teaspoonful powdered cinnamon ; mix thoroughly.   Butter
large custard cups and fill a little more than half
full.   Bake immediately in a quick oven fifteen
minutes.   Serve hot with a sauce of s weetened
cream flavored with sherry wine.

80. SCOTCH CAKE.

One pound sifted flour, three fourths pound
butter, one pound powdered sugar.   Mix into a
dough with three well-beaten eggs ; roll into a thin
sheet cut into round cakes and bake in a quick
oven.   They require but a few minutes.

81. LOAF CAKE.

Six pounds flour, four pounds sugar, three and
three quarter pounds shortening, four eggs, four
nutmegs, two tablespoonfuls mace, one tumbler
cider brandy or three quarters tumbler Santa Cruz
rum ; citron and raisins.

To put it together take one third of the shortening
and sugar and stir to a cream ; add. flour and one
quart yeast.   Wet up with milk about like biscuit ;
let rise over night.   When the rest of the sugar

and shortening are rubbed together and after it is
quite white, add yelks of the eggs and spices and
stir with it.   Let the whole rise two or three hours,
or until light ; then put in pans and bake in not
too hot an oven.   The above rule makes eight
loaves.   For the yeast one quart water, two raw
potatoes, one medium-sized parsnip, raw, a pinch
of hops.   Boil, strain, and work up with distillery
yeast.   Make a day or two before rising.

82. LEMON JELLY CAKE.

One cup of sugar, one cup of milk, three cups
flour, two eggs, two teaspoonfuls of baking powder,
a lump of butter the size of an English walnut,
flavor with extract of lemon; bake in three layers.

Jelly.—Grate the rinds of two large lemons, to
the juice add one cup of sugar, one half cup of
water, one egg, lump of butter; add whole to rinds,
and put on the stove and let it come to a boil; then
thicken with two teaspoonfuls of cornstarch and
spread between layers.

Icing.—Take the white of one egg, and stir in one
half pound of powdered sugar; then flavor with extract of lemon.

83. ALMOND SPONGE CAKE.

Take six eggs, their weight in granulated sugar,
half their weight in flour, one lemon, juice and
grated rind, one cup of finely chopped almonds.
Beat the eggs separately.   Add the sugar to the
thoroughly whipped yelks.   Grate the lemon rind

and strain the lemon juice into this. Now put in half the flour and half the whites, which should be beaten to a stiff froth, then the balance of flour, into which the cup of almonds should be stirred. To prepare the almonds take them from shells, put into a dish and pour boiling water over them till they can be slipped from the skins. Let stand till cold, and then cut them very fine with a sharp knife. Lastly add the remainder of whites of eggs, and beat hard for a few minutes. Have ready two narrow long pans thoroughly greased with sweet lard and heated. Bake twenty-five minutes in a moderate oven.

84. ROYAL FRUIT CAKE.

Take two cups of sugar and one cup of butter, the yelks and whites of four eggs, to be beaten separately, and one cup of milk. Beat butter and sugar to a cream; mix all together with four cups of flour (or sufficient to make a stiff cake dough), into which three heaping teaspoonfuls of good baking powder has been mixed; two cups each of raisins and currants well washed, one quarter of a pound of citron, half pound of figs, one cup each of English walnut and hickory nut meats; chop fine the raisins, figs, citron, and nuts; mix all together and stir well through cake dough. Turn into a well greased pan and bake three hours in a slow oven. Frosting for fruit cake: Three quarters of a pound of powdered sugar, one tablespoonful of water, and three tablespoonfuls of good wine; beat well together, and spread when the cake is cold,

85. BANANA CAKE.

One cup of butter, two cups of sugar, one cup of milk or water, three eggs, four cups of flour, three small teaspoons of baking powder. Mix lightly and bake in layers. Make an icing of the whites of two eggs and one and a half cups of powdered sugar; spread on the layers and cover thickly and entirely with bananas sliced thin. The cake may be flavored with vanilla. The top should be simply frosted.

86. FRENCH CREAM CAKE.

Beat three eggs and one cup of sugar together thoroughly; add two tablespoonfuls of cold water; stir one large teaspoonful of baking powder into a cup and a half of flour; sift the flour in, stirring all the time in one direction; bake in two thin cakes; split the cakes when hot, and fill in the cream prepared in the following manner: To a pint of new milk add two tablespoonfuls of cornstarch, one beaten egg, one half cup of sugar; stir while cooking, and while hot put in a piece of butter, half the size of an egg; flavor the cream with lemon, vanilla, or pineapple, or, if a lover of bananas, slice one or two bananas into it. Frost the cake if liked, but I prefer it without frosting, if eaten while fresh; use a thin blade knife to split the cakes; if the knife is made hot on the stove it will not hurt the cake.

87. SUNSHINE CAKE.

Whites of eleven eggs, yelks of six eggs, one and one half cups of granulated sugar, measured after one sifting; one cup of flour, measured after one sifting; one teaspoonful of cream tartar, one teaspoonful of extract of vanilla. Beat the whites to a stiff froth, and gradually beat in the sugar. Beat yelks in a similar manner. Add to the yelks the whites and sugar, then the flavoring. Mix quickly and well. Bake fifty minutes in a slow oven. Do not grease the pan.

88. SILVER CAKE.

Stir to a cream one cup and a half of powdered sugar, one half cup of butter, add whites of three eggs, beaten stiff, one teaspoon of vanilla or rose, one cup of cold water, three cups of flour, two teaspoons of baking powder; bake in a tin as large as eight by twelve inches, and bake it in a moderate oven.

Frosting.—The whites of two eggs, one pound of powdered sugar; after you have frosted your cake, have some English walnuts cracked, and put half a walnut on each piece of cake; cut the cake in squares.

89. COOKIES.

One egg, one and a half cups of granulated sugar, three fourths cup of butter, three fourths cup of sweet milk, one teaspoonful of cream of tar-

tar, two teaspoonfuls of soda, a little nutmeg, flour
enough so they will roll out good. Have your
oven hot, so they will bake quickly. Without the
soda and cream of tartar the cookies will not be
good.

90. ORANGE CREAM SPONGE CAKE.

Mix, by sifting, three teaspoons of Cleveland's
baking powder with one and a half cups of flour.
In a separate dish beat three eggs until light, add
one and a half cups of white sugar, one half cup of
hot water, and the grated rind of half an orange.
Beat all together and pour into the flour. Stir
thoroughly and bake in layers.

Cream.—One half pint of milk, one egg, one teaspoon of cornstarch, one tablespoon of flour and two
tablespoons of sugar. Heat the milk, beat the
other ingredients together, add and boil until it
thickens. Flavor with the grated rind of the remaining half of the orange, spread between the layers and frost the top with the beaten white of one
egg, and pulverized sugar enough to thicken. A
little of the orange juice may be added to the frosting if desired.

91. GOAT ISLAND CAKES.

These cakes were served at the restaurant on
Goat Island, at Niagara Falls, hence the name.
Beat to a cream two cups of granulated sugar and
one half cup of butter. Add the well beaten yelks
of five eggs and one half cup of cold water. Then

sift in two cups of flour, a pinch of salt and two teaspoonfuls of baking powder. (The two cups of
flour must be measured before sifting.) Beat these
ingredients well, flavor with lemon according to
taste, and lastly, add the whites of the five eggs,
beaten thoroughly. Do not stir long after adding
the whites of the eggs. Bake in gem pans, and
frost if desired.

92. BROWN-STONE-FRONT CAKE.

Whites of four eggs, two cups of sugar, one half
cup of butter, one cup of sweet milk, three cups of
flour, two heaping teaspoons of baking powder
(sifted), one half teaspoon lemon extract. Cream
the butter and sugar, beat the eggs to a stiff froth.
Divide this mixture into two parts. Into one part
put grated chocolate. Bake in two layers in square
tins, one white and one dark cake. Put together
with chocolate frosting, and ice the top with same.
Frosting: Three quarters of a cup each of sugar
and chocolate (grated), a little milk. Cook in basin over the top of the tea kettle. Flavor with
vanilla.

93. LADY-FINGER PUDDING.

One quart of milk, three tablespoonfuls of cornstarch, three tablespoonfuls of sugar, one [tea-
spoonful of extract of vanilla, yelks of two eggs,
little salt, one dozen lady-fingers. Let the milk
come to a boil. Mix the cornstarch, sugar, and
eggs well together; stir them in the boiling milk·
When sufficiently thick, remove from stove and add

the extract of vanilla.   Spread a thin layer of this in the pudding-dish.   Separate the lady-fingers and place a layer of them next, and so on, alternately, until there are about six layers in all.   Add to the whites of the eggs, after beating them to a stiff froth, four tablespoonfuls of sugar.   Spread this over the top and set in the oven until a light brown, then put away to cool before eating.

94. TAPIOCA PUDDING.

Three tablespoonfuls of flake tapioca, cover with two thirds of a pint of water and let stand over night. In the morning place on the stove one quart of milk, with a very small pinch of salt, and when it comes to a boiling point, stir in the tapioca and let the whole boil hard about two minutes; then stir into the pudding-pan, in which you have previously well mixed the yelks of four eggs, with three tablespoonfuls of sugar and sufficient extract of vanilla to flavor; beat whites of the four eggs to stiff froth, add four tablespoonfuls of powdered sugar and a little extract of vanilla, beat up again and spread evenly over the pudding; put in hot oven until slightly browned, which should be about one minute.   Serve cold.

95. RAILWAY PUDDING.

Take one teacupful of powdered sugar, one teacupful of flour, three eggs, one dessert spoonful of baking powder, one ounce of butter, half a dozen drops of essence of almonds, one tablespoonful of milk. Grease thoroughly, with butter, a bread tin; then mix in a large bowl the flour and sugar; add to this the baking powder; break the three eggs in a small bowl and beat them till very light; pour in the milk, drop in the essence of almonds, and when well stirred pour in large bowl, with flour; etc., and stir well; pour the whole in bread tin and put in oven at once. The sauce for the pudding is made as follows: Three ounces of butter, three ounces of powdered sugar, one and a half gills of boiling water, one gill of cherry wine, half a saltspoonful of nutmeg. Beat sugar and butter to a cream in a bowl, pour over this the boiling water, stirring in the meantime; place the mixture in a saucepan and stir over the fire until very hot (not letting it boil), add the wine and nutmeg and the sauce is made.

96. BANANA CREAM PUDDING.

One quart of milk, yelks of three eggs, one large tablespoon of cornstarch, just enough to make a nice thick cream; sweeten to taste (quite sweet); cook; pour over three large bananas, cut in thin slices and laid in the bottom of the dish. Make a meringue of the whites of the eggs and brown in the oven. Set away until cold.

97. PEARL PUDDING.

Half cup of boiled rice, one pint of milk, three tablespoonfuls of sugar, one tablespoonful of corn-starch, one small teaspoonful of salt, and yelks of three eggs. Beat together and cook as a custard.

Put in a dish and allow to cool.　When cool flavor with vanilla.　Beat the whites of the three eggs to a stiff froth; add six tablespoonfuls of sugar; flavor with vanilla, and pour over the pudding.

98. APPLE DUMPLING PIE.

To one pint of rich, sour cream (not bitter) add one teaspoonful of baking soda and a pinch of salt. Stir well till the soda is thoroughly mixed with the cream.　Then stir in enough flour to make a batter thick enough to drop from a spoon.　Pare and slice some mellow tart apples.　Grease your pie tin or tins and spread a layer of the batter over the bottom of the tin, then a layer of the apples, and so alternate till the tin is full, putting in batter last. Put in hot oven (not too hot), and bake till done, which you can tell by trying the dough, as for cake. Cut in pieces and serve with cream and sugar. Flavor the cream, if desired, with nutmeg.　For a large family double the amount of cream.

99. GYPSY PUDDING.

One sheet sponge cake thinly spread with jelly, one glass of wine poured over it; blanched almonds stuck in the cake; pour a boiled custard over the whole.

100. GEM PUDDING.

One quart of milk, yelks of four eggs, one pint bread crumbs, sugar and a little salt.　Put in the oven and bake.　When done, have ready the whites of four eggs beaten to a stiff froth, with one small

cup of powdered sugar and the juice of one lemon.
Spread over the top and put in oven to brown.

101. APPLE CHARLOTTE.

Line a delf dish, which you have carefully rubbed
with a small piece of butter, with slices of bread
cut so as to fit evenly the bottom and sides of the
dish. Pare and slice two quarts of tart, high
flavored apples, enough to nearly reach the top of
the bread. Mix in an eighth of a pound of granulated sugar and a quarter of a pound of butter in
small lumps. Soak a few slices of bread in milk
(all the bread must be free from crust and cut to
match), and cover the apples with the bread, after
having added sufficient cinnamon, mace and nutmeg, one quarter of a teaspoonful of each; fit a
plate close upon the bread, so as to cover and hold
it down. Bake two hours in a very hot oven, and
turn out and serve hot.

102. SUET PUDDING.

One cup sweet milk, one cup chopped raisins,
one cup suet chopped very fine, one cup molasses,
four cups flour, one teaspoon soda; season with
nutmeg and cinnamon and a little salt; to be
steamed in a light covered pail set in a kettle of
boiling water and kept boiling three hours, with the
kettle covered tight. To be eaten with melted
sugar—light brown is best.

103. VANILLA CREAM PUDDING.

One quart sweet cream, yelks of five eggs, one half ounce gelatine, one small cup sugar, two teaspoonfuls vanilla extract.

Preparation.—Soak the gelatine in just enough cold water to cover it for an hour; drain, and stir into a pint of the cream, made boiling hot; beat the yelks with the sugar until smooth and add the boiling mixture, beaten in a little at a time; heat until it begins to thicken, but not boil; remove from the fire and flavor, and while it is still hot, stir in the other pint of cream, whipped to a stiff froth; beat in this "whip," a spoonful at a time, into the custard until it resembles a sponge-cake batter. Dip a mold in ice-cold water, pour in the mixture, and set it on the ice to form.

104. CHOCOLATE PUDDING.

One quart milk set in boiling water, yelks of three eggs, three tablespoons cornstarch, four tablespoons sugar, four tablespoons grated chocolate. Dissolve the cornstarch, beat all well and add to boiling milk. Boil until it bubbles. Put in a deep dish and add teaspoon vanilla extract. Beat the whites of three eggs, add powdered sugar, one teaspoon vanilla. Spread over the top. Set in oven to brown.

105. ROMAN CREAM.

Dissolve half an ounce of gelatine into half a tumbler of boiling water. Then take from the fire and stir in one pint of rich cream, whites of two eggs beaten stiff and stirred in the cream; also one gill of brandy. Flavor to taste and cool in forms.

106. FRUIT PUDDING.

One cup of milk or water, one cup molasses, one cup beef suet, chopped fine; one cup raisins, one teaspoonful soda, one egg, one teaspoonful cloves, two teaspoonfuls cinnamon, one small nutmeg. Stir stiff with flour. Steam three and three quarter hours.

107. PRUNE WHIP.

One pound of best prunes, whites of four eggs, two thirds of a cup of fine granulated sugar, one half pint sweet cream, juice of half a lemon. After the prunes are well washed, stew them till perfectly soft; add sugar while cooking; when cold remove the pits. Whip the whites of the eggs to a stiff froth, adding prunes and lemon-juice, whip all together for ten or fifteen minutes, put into a pudding-dish and bake for twenty minutes in a moderate oven, till a light brown. When very cold serve with the cream, whipped light and slightly sweetened.

108. COFFEE BLANC MANGE.

One quart of milk, one third box of gelatine, one cup of strong coffee, four eggs, one and a half cups sugar. When the milk boils add the eggs and sugar; stir well; then let it come to a boil and add the coffee. Put in a little vanilla, as it is an improvement. Then pour into a large mold or two small ones. This makes enough for eight or ten people.

109. CHOCOLATE BLANC MANGE.

One half box of gelatine, well soaked in half pint cold water. Let one pint and a half of milk come to the boiling point, three quarters of a cup of grated chocolate (not the sweetened), twelve table-spoons sugar; add the gelatine and stir it well a few moments before turning it into the mold; flavor with grated orange peel or vanilla. To be eaten when cold with cream.

110. YANKEE PIE.

To one and one half pounds of best pastry flour allow one and one half pounds of best butter and a little less than three gills of water. Squeeze the butter dry and wring it in a dry napkin free of moisture. Sift the flour into a dry dish. Let every-thing be clean, especially the rolling board and roll-ing pin and the hands. Mix the flour and water in-to a smooth paste, using a clean knife; be careful not to get the paste too wet or it will be tough. Roll out of equal thickness of about an inch. Break about a fourth of the butter into small pieces and place these upon the paste, sift on a little flour, fold over, roll out. Repeat the buttering and roll-ing, dredging to prevent sticking, taking great care to handle and roll very lightly, brushing the paste after each rolling with the white of egg to increase

the quality of flakiness in baking.   Have ready as
soon as the crust is done two quarts of tart, spicy
flavored apples, pared and quartered.   Put one half
of the crust rolled out to the proper size into a
large baking-pan and add the apples, putting in
two cups of sugar.   Place over the apples the upper-
crust, gently compacting and closing the edges.
The oven must be ready to bake at a little more
than medium heat.   As soon as the crust is done
have another baking-pan ready with an under-
crust made of half the quantity of ingredients.   Put
in a layer of apples which are cooked soft.   Break
the thoroughly cooked crust into small pieces and
place a layer of them over the apples, then sprinkle
with sugar, cinnamon and mace.   Add another
layer of soft apples and repeat the spiced layer of
crust with sugar, until all of the cooked crust and
apple are used, taking care to finish with a layer of
apples about one inch thick, which must also be
spiced and sweetened to taste, with a dash of nutmeg, Sprinkle with a few small pieces of butter.
Then the pie is to be returned to the oven long
enough to bake the under-crust.

iii. GREEN APPLE PIE.

The first thing necessary to insure a good pie is
a large, tart apple.   Make a nice, rich pastry of one
third butter and two thirds lard; rub into the flour
lightly and thoroughly.   Add a little salt, and moisten with cold water (if ice-water all the better) by
adding a little at a time until you can press together

for rolling out. Line a medium sized pie-plate with this crust; then peel your apples and slice thin. Fill the plate very full and put the upper-crust on lightly. Bake. When done remove the upper-crust, and with a silver knife mash your apples fine. Mix in one cup of granulated sugar a large spoonful of sweet butter, and nutmeg or lemon to taste. Then replace the upper-crust.

112. MINCE-PIE.

Boil your beef until tender and when cold chop fine. Prepare tart apples by peeling, coring, and chopping fine. Then by measure use double the quantity of apples that you have of beef. If the beef is very lean add one pound of nice suet, chopped fine, to every ten of beef. Then add fruit according to taste and convenience, but be sure to have the mince dark when completed. A can of black raspberries or jam of any kind, some quinces finely chopped, dried cherries or canned ones, raisins seeded and chopped, or plums, add a fine flavor and color. If this entire combination was represented in one "get-up" of mince the flavor would be fine. But there is no iron-clad rule about a mince-pie. You can use the things at hand, only be sure to temper all with good sense and salt. To moisten use a part of the liquor in which the beef was boiled, some boiled cider if you have it, or the liquor from any spiced, sweet, fruit pickle. Nothing is better than this. A little vinegar is generally required to give it tone, and tart, or old cider.

Add molasses and brown sugar, but not so much as to prevent the addition of sugar when the pies are made.

For spice use cloves and cinnamon. Have the whole when put together so moist that it can be readily stirred with a spoon. Place the whole in a pan and set on a kettle of water over the fire, or place in a porcelain kettle and heat gradually until scalding hot. It is then ready to use. A jar filled for winter use is very convenient, and glass fruit cans may be sealed full for summer. To make your pies, rub nice sweet lard into the flour until you can take it into your hand and squeeze into form, which stays nicely together; then add a little salt and moisten with cold water by adding a little at a time, and stirring lightly with a knife until you can take it in your hands and press together for rolling out. Always keep some of the shortened flour to add if a little too moist. Cover your pie tins with crust, then put in the mince as already prepared.

The mince should be so moist as to require a sprinkle of flour over the top. Grate nutmeg over the top of each pie. Place whole raisins over the top; also bits of butter and half a cup of granulated sugar sprinkled evenly over the top of each pie. The upper-crust should have small openings in the centre. Wet the under crust around the edge, that your pie may be properly sealed.

This general rule for making mince-pie has taken the first premium at the largest fairs—without brandy or wine, although they can be added by those who wish them.

113. LEMON MERINGUE PIE.

The grated rind and juice of one lemon, yelks of two eggs, one cup of sugar, two.tablespoons of flour, one cup of milk and a pinch of salt. Line pie plate with crust, pour in the lemon custard and bake from thirty to forty-five minutes. Beat the whites of two eggs to a stiff froth; add one table-spoonful of pulverized sugar. When the pie is baked spread the frosting evenly on top, and stand on the grate in the oven two or three minutes, or until it is slightly browned.

114. PLAIN LEMON PIE.

Grated rind and juice of one lemon, one cup of sugar, one egg. Beat together. Dissolve one table-spoon of cornstarch in a little water, pour on one cup of hot water and cook until it thickens. Then stir in with the egg, sugar and lemon. Make a nice crust of one cup of flour, one third of a cup of lard, pinch of salt. After mixing these thoroughly add a little water and mix as little as possible after the water is added. Bake with two crusts. Wet a piece of cotton cloth an inch wide and put around the edge of the pie to prevent cooking over.

115. SQUASH PIE.

Every one has a way of their own for making pie crust. Line as many deep plates with crust as you wish to make. An egg rubbed over the crust will

keep it from being soggy. For each pie one cup
of sifted squash, one half cup of sugar, one quarter
teaspoonful of cinnamon, one quarter teaspoonful
of nutmeg, one egg and a little salt, two cups of
boiling milk. Beat all together, stir into the milk;
fill the crust and bake. It is better to put your
dish of milk into a kettle of boiling water to boil;
then there is no danger of scorching it. Serve the
pie cold.

116. PUMPKIN PIE.

To one quart of stewed, strained pumpkin add
four well beaten eggs, two quarts of milk, two thirds
of a cup of sugar, and one teaspoonful of ground
nutmeg; beat all well together and bake in a crust
without cover.

For crust, one pound of flour, half a pound of
lard, a little salt, cold water to make into a stiff
dough; this will be enough for four good-sized
pies.

117. CORNSTARCH PIE.

One pint sweet milk, two heaping tablespoons
sugar, yelks of two eggs, quarter of a teaspoon
lemon. Put the mixture in a pail, set in kettle of
water to heat. Mix two tablespoons cornstarch
with a little milk and stir in the mixture in the
pail; cook till it thickens and take from the water.
Pour on a crust which has been previously baked;
cover with frosting made from the whites of two
eggs beaten stiff and mixed with two tablespoons

sugar. Put in oven and brown. This pie ought to be baked in quite a deep plate, and is best to be eaten the same day it is made.

118. APPLE PIE.

One coffee-cup sifted flour; one third coffee-cup lard and butter mixed, sufficient ice cold water to make a soft dough; mix with a knife; roll thin; spread with butter, fold over three times and roll; repeat this for the lower crust, and three or four times for the upper. It should be done as quickly as possible and in a cool place. Fill the pie-pan with nice tart apples sliced very thin, cover with sugar and small pieces of butter, season with cinnamon and nutmeg, add two tablespoons of water, and sprinkle lightly with flour. Just before adding the upper crust dip the fingers in cold water and moisten the edge of the lower crust to prevent the juice from boiling out of the pie.

119. CUSTARD PIE.

Three eggs, three tablespoons sugar, a little salt and cinnamon, one teaspoon melted butter, one pint milk; do not have the oven too hot, and when done set on back of stove to cool before setting away from stove.

120. SPANISH CREAM.

One half box gelatine, one quart milk, five eggs, one cup sugar, flavoring. Soak the gelatine in the milk one hour, then place it on the range, and when at boiling point stir in the well-beaten yolks of the eggs and the sugar; when it is boiling hot remove from the fire and stir in the beaten whites of eggs and flavoring; pour in small molds so that it can be served in dainty individual dishes. This is a very nice dessert.

121. STRAWBERRY SHORTCAKE.

Two heaping teaspoonfuls of baking powder, sifted into one quart of flour, scant half tea-cup of butter, two tablespoonfuls of sugar, a little salt, enough sweet milk or water to make a soft dough; roll out almost as thin as pie crust; place one layer in a baking-pan and spread with a very little butter, upon which sprinkle some flour, then add another layer of crust and spread as before, and so on until crust is all used. This makes four layers in a pan fourteen inches by seven. Bake about fifteen minutes in a quick oven, turn upside down, take off the top layer (the bottom while baking), place on a dish, spread plentifully with strawberries previously sweetened with pulverized sugar, place layer upon layer, treating each one in the same way, and when done to be served warm with cream and sugar. To have light dough, mix it quickly and handle as little as possible. Oranges can be used instead of strawberries; remove the peel and white skin, cut into small pieces, sprinkle with sugar, and let stand a short time before using.

122. OLD FASHIONED GINGER BREAD.

One cup of molasses, half a cup of cold water, half a cup of lard, one teaspoonful of soda, half a teaspoonful of ginger, one fourth of a teaspoonful of salt.

Mix all well together, stir in flour sufficient to roll out; crease by drawing a fork across; cut in squares; bake in a hot oven; the whole depends on good molasses and working soft as possible.

123. APPLE FRITTERS.

Make a batter in proportion of one cup of sweet milk to two cups of flour, a heaping teaspoon of baking powder, two eggs beaten separately, one tablespoon sugar and saltspoon salt; heat the milk a little more than milk-warm. Add slowly to the beaten yelks and sugar, then add flour and whites of eggs; stir all together and throw in thin slices of good, sour apples, dipping the batter up over them; drop in boiling lard in large spoonfuls, with piece of apple in each, and fry to a light brown. Serve with maple syrup or a nice syrup made of sugar.

124. RICE PUDDING.

Boil in a farina kettle one pint of milk, half a cupful of raisins and one cupful of cold boiled rice. When the raisins are cooked stir in the yelks of two eggs, wet with a little milk, salt, spice, and sugar to taste. Let it cook three minutes, pour in a pudding-dish, spread a meringue of the whites on top and brown in the oven. To be eaten cold.

MISCELLANEOUS RECIPES.

125. FRIED OYSTERS.

First dry the oysters, then dip in yelks of eggs well beaten and seasoned, then roll in cracker-dust and lay on a board for fifteen minutes, then dip again in the egg and fry in boiling lard. Serve very hot as soon as dished.

126. OYSTERS AND MACARONI.

One pint of oysters, half cup butter, one and a half cups sweet milk, two eggs, one cup cracker dust, salt to taste; break the macaroni into inch pieces, put it into boiling water and boil twenty minutes; skim it out and put a thick layer of it in the bottom of a buttered pudding-dish; put the oysters and liquor on this with bits of butter and salt; add the remainder of the macaroni; beat the eggs well, mix with the milk, pour over and spread the cracker dust over the top; bake thirty minutes, or less if the oven is very hot; see that it is brown on top.

127. WHITE SOUP.

Take the clear stock of chicken, allowing a gill to a half pint for each person. To one quart of stock add the juice of one small onion, a teaspoonful of salt, half a teaspoonful of pepper, a dash of cayenne, and a tablespoonful of rice previously boiled. Keep over the fire until near the boiling point. Then turn into a soup tureen and serve.

128. CLAM CHOWDER.

Place half a pound of salt pork in three quarts of cold water. Let it boil, then chop four onions and eight potatoes and put in same water. Open ten round clams, chop them fine and place in the stew. Take out the salt pork (which will now be soft enough to chop), chop and add it again to the stew. If the clams are very salt no additional salt will be required. Cook until done, which will be in about one hour, adding more water if it becomes necessary. Just before serving pour boiling milk over four pilot crackers, and when soft add to the chowder. No other crackers will take the place of pilot crackers, and they must be softened in hot milk, to make the best clam chowder known.

129. OX TAIL SOUP.

Take two ox tails and cut them into small pieces; put them into a pot (without any water) until brown, then pour on about one and a quarter gal-

lons of water; add one turnip, a carrot, one onion
cut in small pieces, some celery, parsley, and leek;
also whole pepper and cloves and one can of tomatoes. Let boil slowly for three hours. In the
meantime brown about one cup of flour in oven.
Strain your soup and thicken with the browned
flour, then add one wineglass of claret and one
wineglass of catsup and salt to taste.

130. CORNED BEEF SOUP.

Let seven pounds of cheapest cut of corned beef
be soaked and parboiled so as to remove the sur-
plus salt, then simmer slowly three hours. Let the
liquor stand until all the fat rises. Skim off the
fat. Add a quart of tomatoes, two carrots, two
small white turnips, two onions, and four large potatoes, all pared and sliced thin. Let simmer one
hour. Strain and serve the soup hot, reserving the
cooked vegetables for a salad.

131. SALMON CUTLETS EN PAPILLOTE.

Dry three or four slices of salmon and lay in
melted butter. Dust lightly with pepper and wrap
in well-buttered white paper; stitch down the ends
of each cover. Fry in nice drippings or lard. They
will be done in ten minutes unless very thick. Have
ready clean, hot papers, fringed at the ends; slip
quickly, lest they cool in the process, into the fresh
covers; give the ends a twist and serve on a heated
dish.

132. UNRIVALED CLAM FRITTERS.

Take from the shell twenty-five medium-sized hard shell clams and drain in a colander for a few minutes, after which chop them moderately fine and mix well in a batter made as follows: Take one egg beaten well, five tablespoonfuls sweet milk, pinch of salt, baking soda about the size of a pea, and mix with flour enough to make a thin batter. On a good fire have a pan ready containing equal parts of butter and lard for frying. Drop your fritters in the boiling fat, a tablespoonful of the batter to each, and cook quickly, turning over to brown nicely on both sides. Take out as soon as brown and eat while hot.

133. HOW TO BROIL SHAD.

Shad is the most economical fish we have in the months of April and May. The fish should be split down the back and cooked as fresh as possible. Salt and pepper it well, rubbing it in thoroughly. Place in a wire broiler and cook over a hot fire until well browned, turning but once. Add a few bits of butter when placed upon a hot platter. Serve with fried potatoes.

134. SALMON CROQUETTES.

To a small salmon picked up fine add a large cup of crackers, three eggs well beaten, butter, salt, and pepper. Then moisten with cream to the consistency to roll in shape. Roll in cracker crumbs and fry in very hot fat, as crullers.

135. BAKED RED SNAPPER.

Make a dressing of fine stale bread (that of brown bread of flour of entire wheat is best), season with good butter, pepper, and salt. Fill the fish and fasten the twine. Sprinkle with bits of butter and pepper and salt. Dredge with flour. Bake one hour, or until very tender. Serve with sauce of drawn butter, taking care to keep the large white flakes of the fish from breaking. Garnish with parsley and fried potatoes.

136. CODFISH BALLS.

Cook salt codfish by soaking in water, but do not let it boil. Boil the potatoes and mash. Let both fish and potatoes get thoroughly cold. Use a third more codfish than potatoes. Mix and moisten with a cream gravy made of a large size piece of butter, some milk, and flour to thicken. Form in balls and fry in hot fat.

137. OMELET.

Six eggs, white and yelks beaten separately; half pint milk, six teaspoons corn starch, one teaspoon baking powder, and one teaspoon salt; melt a heaping tablespoon of butter in a frying-pan, and when the mixture has set add the whites, beaten to a stiff froth; cut in two in the center and turn one half over the other before sending to the table.

138. HAM OMELET.

Chop the ham very fine; add twice the quantity of bread crumbs; an egg to each teacupful of the mixture; heat the frying-pan, and have ready some melted butter to fry without sticking; put in the mixture like large, thin pancakes, molding into shape with a spoon; when brown turn carefully.

139. EGG SALAD.

Boil hard one dozen fresh eggs. When cold, chop fine, with the stalks and tender leaves of a large root of celery and a large handful of fresh green parsley. Pour over the mixture a sauce made by rubbing together a dessert spoonful of mustard, with the same quantity of salt and two spoonfuls of granulated sugar, into which beat well five spoonfuls of olive oil and seven of vinegar.

140. FRITTERS.

Two eggs, well beaten, two tablespoons melted lard, two thirds cup sweet milk, one heaping tea-spoon baking powder, little salt and flour to make a stiff batter; drop from a spoon (small) into hot lard; let cook to a nice brown; try with broom splint to tell when thoroughly done. To be eaten with maple syrup or melted sugar.

141. CORN STARCH PATTIES.

Take one teacupful powdered sugar, one teacupful corn starch, two eggs, one teaspoonful of cream of tartar, one half teaspoonful of soda, three tablespoonfuls of sweet milk, three tablespoonfuls of melted butter, two tablespoonfuls of flour; flavor with lemon extract. Bake in pattie pans; take from oven, and while hot sprinkle with powdered sugar.

142. OLD FASHIONED WAFFLES.

Two quarts of milk, six eggs, one pound butter, a bowl sponge, little salt. If you want them for 6 o'clock dinner or tea, make your sponge 11 A.M., and for this take one and a half pints water, stir flour in until stiff, dissolve one yeast cake (compressed), and stir in also, cover with plate and stand in warm place. As soon as light (which will be very soon after dinner) mix your waffles. Use a large stone pot, same size top and bottom. Have milk warm, butter soft enough to mix well, and eggs beaten; pour all in stone pot, also sponge; stir in flour until considerable thicker than gridle cakes, stand in warm place, and when light are ready to bake in a waffle iron. For a sauce, heat milk with a little butter in, cover each waffle with powdered sugar and pour over the hot milk. This is the old-fashioned Dutch way of making waffles.

143. ENGLISH BANBURY CAKES.

Rub two thirds of a cup of lard through two cups of flour with a pinch of salt, then add about a half cup of water; stir together with a knife; do not mix. Roll out as for pie crust and cut out with a quart oyster pail cover, or about four inches in diameter. Filling—One cup of seeded raisins, rind and juice of one lemon, one cup sugar, five figs. Chop figs and raisins, mix all together, and put a teaspoonful on each round of paste, wet the edges and lap one side of the paste over, pinch the edges together and stick holes in the top of each with a fork. Bake from twenty minutes to one half hour. This recipe makes one dozen and a half of cakes.

144. PEACH TROJA.

Line a glass dish with lady fingers, fill in with ripe peaches, pared and cut small, or sliced. Whip half a pint of cream till firm, spread over the peaches. Serve with cream sweetened and flavored with vanilla.

145. SHERRY JELLY.

One-quarter package of gelatine, one cup of fine white sugar, one wine-glass of good sherry. Dissolve the gelatine in two cups and a half of warm water (not hot) by putting it over the steam of a tea kettle or in a pan of hot water, stirring all the

time. When dissolved add sugar and strain
through a cloth; when cold put in the sherry and
whip for fifteen minutes with a good egg beater;
turn into a glass dish. It is best to make it the
night before needed, so it may be well set, although
not intended to be in a solid mold.

146. MINCE MEAT.

One cup chopped meat, one and a half cups
raisins, same of currants, same of brown sugar,
one cup granulated sugar, one third cup molasses,
three cups chopped apples, one cup meat liquor;
two teaspoonfuls salt, same of cinnamon, half
teaspoonful mace, same of cloves, one lemon,
chopped; quarter pound citron, half cup brandy,
quarter cup wine, half pint jelly.

Do not put in the brandy and wine until meat is
cooked. Cider and vinegar can be used in place of
brandy and wine if preferred. Use a piece of solid
lean meat cut from the round. As the apples vary
in flavor it is best to season to taste. This makes
four pies.

147. TONGUE OR HAM SANDWICHES.

Chop fine the lean of cold boiled tongue or ham,
season with prepared mustard and black pepper,
add melted butter and sweet cream until smooth
like a paste, then spread between buttered slices of
bread.

148. MAYONNAISE SAUCE.

Mix in a large bowl one teaspoonful each of mustard and salt with one and a half of vinegar; beat in the yolk of one raw egg and gradually beating meanwhile a half pint of the best quality of sweet olive oil until the mixture become a thick, even batter. This may be kept closely covered in a cold place for many weeks, and when used may be flavored with fresh lemon juice or a little vinegar. It is the most delicious of all salad sauces.

149. WELSH RAREBIT.

Cut off the crusts of thin slices of bread and toast to a nice brown. Spread with butter and cover with thin slices of rich cheese. Spread over with a little prepared mustard and put in the oven until the cheese is soft. Then cut in pieces and serve immediately on hot dishes.

150. QUAILS ROASTED WITH HAM.

Clean, truss and stuff as usual. Cover the entire bird with thin slices of corned ham or pork and wrap with a sheet of white paper, binding with buttered thread. Baste frequently with butter and water that they may not burn. Roast three quarters of an hour. Remove the papers and meat before sending to table and brown quickly.

151. CARAMEL OR BURNT SUGAR.

For coloring soups, sauces, and gravies, put one cup sugar and two teaspoonfuls water in a saucepan on the fire. Stir constantly until it is quite a dark color, then add a half cup water and a pinch of salt. Let it boil a few minutes and when cold bottle.

152. LAMB CHOPS (BROILED.)

Take rib chops, wipe with a damp cloth, place in a tin; salt and pepper them and put into oven, letting them remain until done through. Then take them and place on broiler just long enough to brown nicely. When done place on platter; butter them and serve. Do not have your fire too hot, as it is apt to burn them. I also cook "Broiled Chicken" in this way.

153. ROAST BEEF.

Buy the second cut of beef, say about six to eight pounds. Have your butcher trim it and make into a round, holding it in place with wooden skewers. Salt well; put in spider; place in oven, which should be of an even heat. When it becomes hot enough to "hiss," put in a little warm water. It will take from two to two and a half hours to roast a piece of meat this size. Be sure and keep water enough in spider, else your meat will burn and stick to

your spider, making your gravy (if you use it) un-
fit for use.   I am not obliged to baste my meat, as
my range cooks the meat very tender and retains
all the juices.   While I am not writing up the
merits of different stoves, I do wish all housekeep-
ers could see for themselves the advantages the
range with a gauze oven-door posseses over other
ranges.

154. TO COOK ASPARAGUS.

Scrape the stems of the asparagus lightly, but
very clean.   Throw them into cold water, then tie
in bunches of equal size.   Cut the large ends evenly, that the stems may be all of the same length,
and put the asparagus into plenty of boiling water,
with a little salt while it is boiling; cut slices of bread
half inch thick, pare off the crust and toast it a delicate brown on both sides.   When the stalks of the
asparagus are tender, lift it out directly, or it will
lose its color and flavor, and will be liable to break.
Now dip the toast quickly into the liquor in which
the asparagus was boiled, and dish the asparagus
upon it with the points meeting in the center.
Pour over rich melted butter, and serve hot.

155. ROAST MUTTON WITH TOMATOES.

Take one nice hindquarter of mutton, wash it,
rub it with salt and pepper, put it into a baking-pan
with a pint of water, and baste it well.   Then prepare some tomatoes in the following manner;

Take one dozen large, full, ripe tomatoes. Slit them into four, but do not sever the pieces entirely at the bottom. Make a stuffing of some bread, crumbs, pepper, salt, butter and a very little sugar. Mix it well, remove part of the seed from the tomatoes, and fill with the stuffing; put them in and roast with the mutton. When done put them in the dish around the mutton and pour over some gravy. Tomatoes done in this manner make a delicious accompaniment to all kinds of cooked meats.

156. BROILED STEAK.

Have your steak cut about three fourths or one half inch in thickness, place the gridiron over clear fire and rub the bars with fat; place the beefsteak on it and broil, turning frequently, carefully picking fork through fat, for if the steak itself is pricked gravy will run out, and it will harden. Have ready a hot dish on which you have placed a lump of butter size of large walnut; when done lay on hot dish, rub with butter, and serve as quickly as possible.

157. MUTTON CHOPS BROILED.

Cut some chops from the best end of the loin, trim neatly, removing the skin or fat, leaving only enough fat to make them palatable; place the chops on a gridiron over a very clear fire; turn them frequently, taking care that the fork is not put into the lean part of the chop. Season with pepper and salt. When done put a piece of fresh butter over each chop, and send them to the table on a hot dish; time, 10 minutes to cook.

158. SUCCOTASH.

Take six ears of nice tender corn, cut off grains from cob, and mix with one pint of young Lima beans; after boiling them well in salt and water, drain through a colander and place at once into a pan-cover to keep hot. Have ready two eggs well beaten with one ounce of butter; pour this mixture over the corn and beans, adding pepper and salt to taste. Serve hot.

159. BOILED HAM.

Take a ham, say of ten or twelve pounds, pour boiling water over it, and let it cool enough to wash and scrape it clean; put in a large kettle, cover with cold water; let boil a minute, then place it on the back part of the stove to let simmer steadily six hours. Be careful to keep the water at a low point, and do not allow it to get much above it. Turn the ham over once or twice. Remove the skin from the ham when done, set in the oven, placing the lean side downward; sift over powdered crackers and bake one hour: this brings out a quantity of fat, leaving the ham more delicate, and it will keep much longer in warm weather,

160. MUTTON CHOPS, BROILED.

Select good fat chops from the fore-quarter, cut thick; remove the bone from one and press the meat closely to the other; also trim off the meat from the small part of the bone two or three inches, to serve as a handle. Broil over a brisk fire of charcoal, turning frequently until done to fancy. Serve on a hot platter and garnish the chops by neatly wrapping around the handle of each clear white paper, and lay a sprig of fresh celery-top on each chop.

VEGETABLES.

161. STUFFED CABBAGE.

Cut out the heart of a large cabbage by spreading back the leaves—to do which without breaking, pour over it boiling water; fill the vacancy with finely chopped and cooked veal or chicken, and roll in balls with the yolk of eggs. Tie it firmly together, and boil in a covered kettle two hours.

162. FRIED SQUASH.

Slice the squash thin, fry slowly in butter and lard, being very careful not to let it stick to the pan; brown nicely on each side, remove to a warm platter, put butter, salt, and pepper over it. Serve hot.

163. BAKED ONIONS.

Wash the onions, but do not peel; put in a sauce pan cover with salted water; boil an hour, replacing the water with more boiling water as it evaperates; turn off the water and lay the onions on a cloth to dry them well; roll each one in a piece of buttered tissue paper, twisting it at the top to keep it on, and bake in a slow oven one hour; brown slightly, basting well with butter, for fifteen minutes; season with salt and pepper, and pour some melted butter over them.

PASTRY.

164. CREAM PIE.

To each pie, one cup sugar, three eggs, these thoroughly beaten with a little salt and nutmeg, one cup of sweet cream, using sweet milk to finish filling the crust.

Pie crust.—Allow to each pie one cup sifted flour, a small pinch of salt, one fourth teaspoon baking powder, one large tablespoon lard. Pour your cold water in,—ice-water if you have it, a little at a time, and be sure not to over-wet the flour. Do not mould or handle it but mix with a knife, and roll it out soft as possible. Slow oven is essential in pie baking.

163. CLAM FRITTERS.

One egg, one-half cup milk, one teaspoon baking-powder, one cup flour, twelve hard-shell clams chopped fine. Stir all together, and fry in hot fat same as crullers.

Omit the clams, and use, with the above, one pint greencorn chopped fine, one half teaspoon pepper, one half spoon salt, one half teaspoon sugar, and small tablespoon butter. Fry in the same manner.

164. CHICKEN PIE.

Just as your husband's "mother used to make it."

Cut into pieces and boil, four chickens. Remove the larger bones—all of them. Cook in sufficient water to make plenty of gravy, and leave it on the boiled chicken. Add salt and pepper to taste. Thicken the gravy with a couple of tablespoons of flour well blended with a little cold water. Leave no lumps of flour.

This will fill your pie, which must be baked in a four-quart pudding-dish. (Though if you use a tin pan, it will look more like "mother's.") Now for the crust.

One and a half quarts flour in your sieve, five teaspoons (pretty full) of Royal Baking Powder, teaspoon salt. Sift all together once or twice. Then rub into flour a cup of butter. Then with a spoon mix a soft batter with milk. Mix it so soft you can just barely mix afterwards with hands and roll out. Roll one half of it about half an inch thick, and line your dish; be sure and let the crust come well up around and over the edge of the dish. Now put in your chicken, and cover with the remainder of the crust about the same thickness, and cover. Pinch the edges firmly together and on your top crust make the "quirly " flower mother used to put on. Bake an hour in a quick oven. Let stand fifteen or twenty minutes before sending to table. Then don't put onto your table a great variety of other good things to spoil the pie; and if you can by some means find for your good man the appetite he brought home from school with him when a healthy, hearty, growing boy, and sat down with a dozen others, ready to devour whatever was set before him, I venture to say he'll enjoy that pie and declare it was " almost as good as mother's."

IMPORTANT NOTICE.

The PRESS prints NEW recipes in its Daily, Sunday and Weekly Editions regularly.

ARE YOU THINKING ABOUT
BUILDING A HOUSE?

If you are, you ought to buy the new book, *Palliser's American Architecture,* or every man a complete builder, prepared by Palliser, Palliser & Co., the well known architects.

There is not a Builder or any one intending to Build or otherwise interested that can afford to be without it. It is a practical work and everybody buys it. The best, cheapest and most popular work ever issued on building. Nearly four hundred drawings. A $5 book in size and style, but we have determined to make it meet the popular demand, to suit the times, so that it can be easily reached by all.

This book contains 104 pages 11 x 14 inches in size, and consists of large 9 x 12 plate pages giving plans, elevations, perspective views, descriptions, owners' names, actual cost of construction, *no guess work,* and instructions *How to Build* 70 Cottages, Villas, Double Houses, Brick Block Houses, suitable for city suburbs, town and country, houses for the farm and workingmen's homes for all sections of the country, and costing from $300 to $6,500; also Barns, Stables, School House, Town Hall, Churches, and other public buildings, together with specifications, form of contract, and a large amount of information on the erection of buildings, selection of site, employment of Architects. It is worth $5.00 to any one, but I will send it in paper cover by mail postpaid on receipt of $1.00; bound in cloth, $2.00.

Address all orders to J. S. OGILVIE, PUBLISHER,
P. O. Box 2767. 57 Rose St., New York.

Ogilvie's Pocket Manual and Universal
ASSISTANT.
CONTAINS
One Million Useful Facts and Figures.
IT IS WORTH $5.00 BUT COSTS ONLY 25 CENTS.

The times are peculiarly calculated to increase every person's desire to *make* and *save money.* New and improved management of business and financial affairs, and economy in daily expenses of all kinds, are the universal study. And almost everyone has felt the need—the great and pressing need, sometimes—of *a concise and throughly* PRACTICAL hand book, calculated to aid him in his plans of thrift and management. Especially is there a demand for a *low-priced* volume of this character, for the self-education of young men and young women for the *realities* of life on the farm, and in the counting-room, the workshop, and the household.

To meet this great popular want, this valuable work has been prepared. It is a remarkable book. It contains a larger amount of valuable information on *practical* matters, *in shape for ready use,* than can be bought in any other form for **$15.00,** yet is sold at only **25 cents.** It is *invaluable* to Every Farmer, Every Mechanic, Every Workman, Every Book-keeper, Every Tradesman, Every Machinist, Every Clerk, Every Investor, Every Land Owner, Every Housekeeper, Every Professional Man, Every Letter Writer, Every Patentee, Every Author, in fact no person who can read the English language should be without a copy of it. Bound in limp cloth, **25 cents;** heavy silk cloth, **50 cents.**

Send 25 Cents at once for a sample copy and agents terms.

It contains about 250 pages and is for sale by every newsdealer and bookseller in the United States, and on all trains, or it will be sent by mail, postpaid, on receipt of price, by

J. S. OGILVIE, PUBLISHER,

P. O. Box 2767.   57 Rose Street, New York.

OGILVIE'S FIRESIDE READING.

◁ A COMPLETE STORY IN EACH NUMBER. ▷

Single Copy 5 Cents. J. S. OGILVIE, Publisher, 57 Rose Street, New York. 50 Cents. Per Year.

I desire to call your attention to this new publication offering complete stories at the nominal price of five cents each.

Each number is bound in handsome paper cover and contains a complete story by a popular American or English Author, among whom are May Agnes Fleming, "Author of Dora Thorne," Charles Dickens, Charles Reade, Mrs. O. F. Walton, "Author of A Bad Boy's Diary," William Black, Mary Cecil Hay.

The following stories (complete) are in the first six numbers:

No. 1. **Fated to Marry.**
　　　By MAY AGNES FLEMING.
" 2. **Blunders of a Bashful Man.**
　　　By "AUTHOR OF A BAD BOY'S DIARY."
" 3. **Ninety-Nine Recitations and Readings.**

No. 4. **The Lost Bank Note.**
　　　By Mrs. HENRY WOOD.
" 5. **Wedded and Parted.**
　　　By "AUTHOR OF DORA THORNE."
" 6. **Christie's Old Organ.**
　　　By Mrs. O. F. WALTON.

All who read choice fiction can at once see the advantage of this publication over those which have continued stories from week to week or from month to month, as in this publication *every story is complete*, and they are not *short sketches*, but stories which if issued in regular book form would make from 180 to 350 pages each. *Price of each number, only 5 cents.* It is issued monthly. Sold by all booksellers and newsdealers, or mailed to any address on receipt of price by

J. S. OGILVIE, Publisher,

57 Rose Street, New York.